Bit

Living the Dream On G Wing

By Sheila Cooper

To the men and women who walk the landings with courage, honour and pride

LIVING THE DREAM ON G WING

<u>Warning</u>

This publication contains adult content
and strong language.

A light-hearted but serious insight into the first few weeks of life as a prison officer, as seen through the eyes of a new recruit.

A spit in the face from someone, or a slice from a concealed weapon. It's an accepted risk, simply to keep the establishment free from any contraband, as that would have a huge impact on the safety of prisoners and staff alike. The officers try and make the transition as inoffensive as possible and most of the time, a good rapport is built within that first hour. It's a skill like no other and even whilst the bewildered men are getting presented with ill-fitting, dull, grey and often itchy clothing, their heavy moods typically subside; and they become settled. They begin the new entry process and are led customarily carrying their neat bundles of prison issue bedding; to bunk up in unfamiliar, bare and colourless units, with an individual they have never met. Indeed, their very first night in a custody setting must be daunting to say the least.

The characters in this book are purely fictitious and any resemblance to anyone living or dead is completely unintentional and totally coincidental

Published 2020.   *RRP. £9.99*

Chapter 1

Into The Unknown

Chapter 1

Into The unknown

Quite often as the new inmates step down from intimidating white vans, jaded from long and uncomfortable journeys hidden behind blackened windows; before being incarcerated into the grey bleakness of the prison, I find myself studying them, and I can't help wondering what the boundaries are between shame and desire.

The hoards of innocuous reflections, that can relate to an individual story in several diferent ways. Some of the explanations seem reasonable and probable, but, no one buys the usual bullshit stories, that flow effortlessly from implausible lips; as the eyes shine brightly in total contrast to the words being spoken. Words, so urgent and willing you to believe in them, that the credibility becomes lost.

Many masquerade as heavy gangsters but some were so fragile, they fell apart at the onset of their sentence. There are very few words to describe the failed concealment of the anguish in some of the young eyes; as they realise the magnitude of their loss of liberty as it hits home. Or the first wave of reaction, as the cell door slams shut for the very first time.

There was often a fair amount of hostility, that increased at first, particularly with the ones that couldn't face being arrested and detained. Unfortunately, as the initial act of searching is pretty invasive, it comes as quite a shock and it has to be, by it's very nature. However, it's very necessary and is paramount to the security and wellbeing of others. I couldn't count the times I have heard the classic phrase of. "Fuck off you bastards, what do you think you are doing, you are invading my privacy. Hey, now, you are sexually abusing me, I'll have my solicitor on you all for this!" followed by countless unheard of obscenities. We have to find anything they may be concealing, as if it gets out on to the wings, the fallout could be devastating. We stand back as much as possible, but, we can't distance ourselves from the detained men and their outbursts. We simply have to remain still and take it and so do they!

Sometimes it can be unrelenting, we try our utmost to communicate in an effective manner, however, it's like trying to reach out underwater. Sometimes it's urgent and the men need immediate help, they are not as tough as they think they are, and they can often arrive in crisis, and it's in those initial moments you refrain from confronting them; as after all, who knows what had really transpired to bring them into a prison. Whatever people think, our job is simply to look after them and make sure they are kept safe and well whilst they are in our care, and, of course, it stands to reason, that our patience and integrity must be paramount, if they are to learn to trust us.

It's a rude awakening to be sure as the first experience of prison life must be so daunting and however hard the exterior of an individual may appear to those they do not know; there will always be just that tiny little element that will contradict their veracity so there is always a unique clue. It's something you only learn to read through experience and it separates them from the rest. These are the ones you have to watch, take care of and help to support, as, these are the lost and confused souls that need looking after; they are the ones you feel the most sorry for: The ones that have empty eyes and vacant hearts.

It must be pretty depressing, I suppose. In fact it's a cold and hard dose of reality and a proper scare, to be lined up, waiting for your turn to be taken to one side and body searched. The routine order to, "Squat!" within earshot of others. The poking and the prying, the clumsy intrusion into body cavities without emotion or humility. Some take it in their stride but some are humiliated by it. Then there are the un-fortunate officers, who can find that they are occasionally forced to put themselves in danger, of a getting a scratch from a hidden needle, or a severe infection from bodily fluids, should an examination glove break on someone with hepatitis, or HIV or similar.

A spit in the face from someone, or a slice from a concealed weapon. It's an accepted risk simply to keep the establishment free from any contraband, as that would have a huge impact on the safety of prisoners and staff alike. The officers try and make the transition as inoffensive as is possible and most of the time a good rapport is built within that first hour. It's a skill like no other and even whilst the bewildered men are getting presented with ill-fitting, dull, grey and often itchy clothing, their heavy moods typically subside and they become settled. They begin the new entry process and are led customarily carrying their neat bundles of prison issue bedding; to bunk up in unfamiliar, bare and colourless units with an individual they have never met. Indeed, their very first night in a custody setting must be daunting to say the least.

We understand that we constantly have to deal with all sorts of people who act and think so differently from us, but, we also know that sometimes, it simply isn't their fault and although we stand together, we also feel sympathy for the unfortunate and underpriviliged indiiduals. Whatever they did on the outside is not our business, it's our business to look after them on the inside, it's as simple as that. Sometimes the newcomers are packed like bean bags, their backsides must hurt like holy hell, but, everything is available at a price and he lads will constantly try their luck for a quick few quid, especially if they come back in to us on a recall. The contraband they are urged to try to bring in, is worth a small fortune in the right hands, inside, and they obviously feel that the risk is worth it. They just think it's a game, they laugh and say laws are there to be broken and they take it on the chin when it goes wrong. I like to think that not much gets through the system but it stands to reason that nothing is infallible, some of these boys are very clever and others are simply desperate. They don't care about putting themselves in harms way. Their lives and those of their families; were quite often dependent on them successfully bringing in their illicit contraband. Their stories are complex and they ride a rocky road.

There are so many extraordinary pressures and ill-considered expectations, some with such unrealistic deadlines. Prison officers are only human after all, and sometimes the work can take its toll on their physical and mental health. You develop a deep rooted instinct to look out for yourself, your colleagues, and your mates, and if someone doesn't seem to be their usual self, well, they are probably not; so, it's essential to take some time to ask them if they are ok. The job tends to do that to you, and its imperative to keep things in check. It's vitally important to notice any changes, it's what keeps us rational and bound tightly in our comradeship.

Chapter 2

A New Day

Chapter 2

A New Day

Groups of officers, dressed in the familiar black and white, streamed in orderly lines towards the imposing wooden gates, that would take them through the bleak grey walls of HMP Scupton; and then into the hidden environment, that only those that knew it could comprehend. The forgotten front liners eminent in all their smartness; their partly concealed chains glistening in the morning sun, giving a covert little clue to their formidable roles.

These exceptional individuals, obviously took pride in their uniforms, as their boots were highly polished and their shirts were crisp and white. Their faces scrubbed and eager, showed determination and resolve. All in all, it was commendable to see that most of them showed such great dignity in their appearance, as well as in their chosen profession. The officers are an interesting bunch to say the least as there are so many distinct idiosyncrasies. Some walked tall and straight, some hurried and worriedly glanced at their wrist-watches. A few were shouting and play-fighting and some just dawdled along, as if they had all the time in the world, pausing only for a quick drag on a cigarette before disappearing through the heavy gates.

Once inside, there was an organized chaos of purposeful shuffling towards the key-locks and the radio cabinets. Phones were held frantically aloft, as each officer tried their hardest, to get their hands on one of the limited lockers before they all got used up. If they were unlucky, they would have the inconvenience of running back to their cars with their lifelines, then starting their day harassed.

Mobile phones are obviously banned from within the walls, they are not allowed past the gate but the officers insist on bringing them in, then bellyaching because there's nowhere to put them. It's beyond me, as I just leave mine in the car and check it on my tea-break, it's not worth the hassle.

It was the typical change of shift chaos, with the free for all banter and loud back slapping. There was the regular grumbling and calling for the entrance to be unlocked quicker and there was a chaotic, infantile but harmless bitch-fest; such as you can expect in such a confined space, filled to the brim with a mixture of contrasting personalities. The early morning rush was indisputably stressful enough; without the altogether miserable, loud and impatient characters becoming quarrelsome. Then there were the nominal negativity sharers, protesting their woes and gripes to anyone who would listen. There were those that liked to start the day on a negative and soulless note reaching out for sympathy, but, not many ears showed much interest in their whingeing so they moaned and grizzled about everyone and everything around them instead.

Officer Noel did a fart and caused raucous badgering from his closest peers and the girls held their noses, swiped the air and called him a stinking twat. When the door was finally opened, everyone tumbled out into the yard and took immediate flight across the grey tarmac in a scuffle, and not only to get away from the pungent smell that grossly offended the nostrils of every-one in the vicinity, but to get to the coffee vending machine first.

The board room was particularly crowded that morning, the Governor had asked for all available staff to be present. Not many seats were available, so I sat myself along-side Officer Simpson, he was never one to mince his words and he constantly made it his business to run down the wives and girlfriends of everyone else. We assumed that it was most probably due to jealousy, because he didn't have a partner himself.

However, for whatever reason ensued; he seemed obsessed with everyone else and how their relationships were progressing, particularly with regard to how often they were bonking, or not, whichever the case may be. He grabbed every opportunity to voice his own opinion on sexuality and I inwardly cringed and secretly wished that he didn't like me. Then, as if my choice of seating hadn't been a bad enough call, I heard the sound of Officer Bill Cannon's irritating laugh to the left of me, as usual he was gossiping about one of the newest young recruits. I don't know how he got his information but I'm sure he makes a lot of it up.

"Aye, he went from zero to pissed in five minutes flat, poor bastard, still hasn't got the slightest clue it was me that nicked his keys. I bet his wife went fucking mad. At least she let him go out for a change, but, l'll tell you what, he's got some serious bloody issues with that woman! Christ almighty; a fucking good shag, she needs, that's for sure: She can't be getting it at home, can she? She wouldn't be such a bloody miserable old witch, if she was! Fuck me, if my wife was like that I'd have moved out years ago!"

I really think it would be to everyone's benefit, if a new law was created, so that Officer Cannon and Officer Simpson were forced to sit together, as far away from everyone else as possible and banned from saying a freaking word! They were both a bloody nuisance. Perhaps someone should have a word with one of the Governors about them. I leaned back in my chair and scanned the room, it dawned on me that everyone appeared to be looking pretty upset and frustrated; there was something going on, something must have happened before the last shift had ended. A highly charged atmosphere was emanating from the approaching group of senior officers so I decided that it was probably not the most convenient time, to start whingeing like a spoiled little baby.

Officer Llewellyn piped up, that a lad on G Wing had swallowed some batteries and he knew of someone else who had done exactly the same thing and had become seriously ill after doing it. Gaynor, from the procurement office looked extremely interested and questioned him on it and he said "Oh aye, yes, I knew it, as soon as I saw him because he was looking a little bit bright." Gaynor didn't seem to get the wise-crack and everyone fell about in fits of laughter at her expense. Bless her, she was so literal and she never got any of the jokes. After five minutes trying to explain it to her we gave up.

For some reason, the Governor was a bit late coming in and most of the officers sat fidgeting on the edges of the hard plastic chairs, waiting for their morning briefing. The customary individuals all sat in their friendly little clicks hunched over their hot coffee. Some were yawning like demented hippos and some were struggling not to, with obvious, undisguised embarrassment, and a number were trying their hardest to keep awake and alert.

Others were preoccupied in animated conversation. Then there were the usual noisy and boisterous ones, the ones I wanted to scream: "Will you all, shut the fuck up," to, as they pissed around with their loud and childish behavior. Fair play, they were a very unique and interesting crowd, and, although some of them got on my nerves, I still loved their tenacity.

The officer in charge was in fine form and as usual, he could hack the ribbing down with a single quip: "You lot, can cut the twaddle and those of you that are finding it hard to keep awake, be warned, I'm not promising not to cut your dicks off in your sleep!" The intense look in his eyes was murderous. He slaughtered me, he was so funny, but by God he was so scary. I was terrified of him and I wasn't the only one.

The mood soon became somewhat muted and serious, as it became evident that the previous night had been an absolutely lousy one. It hadn't been just the normal busy night routine with intermittent spats of the usual unnecessary nonsense, from a small handful of the unruly prisoners who thought it was fun to wind up the officers. There had actually been quite a serious incident and one of the duty officers had ended up in hospital. Indeed, it was no joke and the Governor had not been in the mood for any of the flippant banter. The alpha male had unleashed the darkest force inside him, with his call for quiet. "Oh here we go!" I thought it best to get the hell to the back of the meeting room, as I had no desire to be volunteered for any of his fancy plans for the remainder of the shift! For my own sanity, I, at least, wanted to counterbalance the unfairness of catching his gaze.

I was totally convinced that the Number I Governor may be living in some sort of alternative world to ours, as, for Christ's sake, no one spoke like that these days but off he went on one of his strict lectures. He sounded like William Shakespeare on speed and was giving evil eyes to anyone who had the gall to cough, or sneeze, or in any other way foolishly distract him from his magnificent delivery.

"The existence of criminality and need for keeping it contained, is the responsibility of us all, and as proud representatives of Her Majesty's prison service, it is our task and indeed our duty to cause these things not to happen and keep in control of any situation at hand. The intent last night was to cause as much chaos as possible and it was a mission to disrupt the establishment and destroy our spirit. We have identified the ringleaders and good work to all those wearing the body-cams. The evidence is irrefutable and all the men involved have been put on full report. Now, I expect the utmost vigilance from you all.

When you create a doorway and allow the release of negative forces, you may not be surprised at the knock on effect it will have on us all. The safety of my officers is paramount!" He kept the lecture going for at least fifteen minutes, then, ended with: "And I have had a lot to explain to those above, in fact, it was one of the roughest meetings I have ever had to attend. I'm running a one man show here and I can't let us flounder."

I wished the Governor well on his journey of self-importance and found myself away with the fairies until Officer Potter nudged me so hard, that I had to rub my shoulder. "Gov's looking out for volunteers to do bed-watches over the weekend. I could do with the overtime, you up for it? Daniel is doing it and Jake from A wing!"

Officer Jackson leaned over me, he stank of B.O. and he looked like he had been up all night. "Bloody bed-watches, for Christ sake don't go on one with Daniel; he slept all sodding night but when Sparky nodded off for a few minutes in the morning, he took a fucking picture on his mobile and reported him. Watch that twat, he's out for himself, there's a fucking invisible ladder hanging out of the C.M.'s arse-hole and

Daniel is ready to climb up it on the way to the number one's office."

"Aye, he's heading for Governors status and his brown nosing face is already so far up the big bosses' backsides, he's got shit in his ears!"

Despite his whiffy armpits everyone really loved Jackson, as he was incredibly funny and always managed to cheer us up with his manic wit; particularly during a night shift, when he would entertain us with his crazy stories. The lads actually went and bought him some soap on a rope and some Lynx Africa last Christmas, but, they are probably still untouched in the freaking packaging, as he's not one to take a hint.

"Hey, look at Stuart, the smug little shit, he said he shagged Imogen last night, he hasn't got the biggest hammer in the tool-box, but, he can nail the women ha ha," The Number one rested his eyes on him and directed his voice towards him. "That reminds me, Jackson, well done, talking about tool boxes, perhaps you can report to the works department during your lunch hour, I believe they are in need of a hand fixing the drain outside the laundry and the guttering behind A Wing."

Jackson mumbled a slightly embarrassed: "Sorry Gov!" then sat back quietly on his chair for the remainder of the meeting. He had now really buggered up his lunchtime stroll down to the new burger bar with the boys. He was risking it, and he knew it. It really wasn't a very good idea to go and unleash the Governor's wrath, particularly when he had an avid audience and he was now a marked man.

All briefed up for their shifts, the officers dispersed to their relevant work-stations and the Governor took Jackson aside. I caught up with him, later, and he told me he had been given a proper grilling. "Oh my freaking God, that's decided it now!" Jackson pointed to the ground. "There's no hell down there, hell is here, this is hell right here, hell on earth. He's only got me helping out on works all bloody afternoon and I've got to wear a boiler suit and a sodding filter mask! Shit! I'm going to be walking around like frosty the fucking snowman. The boys are going to just love giving me stick over this!" I gave him a quick hug and advised him where to find some marigolds and to be far more careful in future, before legging it away in fits of laughter. Meanwhile, Jackson sloped off grudgingly to the works office to collect his gear.

Chapter 3

Stringing Along

Chapter 3

Stringing Along

The lads up on the top landing of D Wing, had each torn away the edges of of their sheets and strung them together, to make sort of lassoos, which they had then used to swing their smuggled contraband from window to window. It was an effectively, silent and convenient way of spreading their merchandise. It was a big headache for the officers, as there was the alarming and added concern that ripped bed-sheets have sometimes, very sadly, been used to make a noose.

The very fabric of the material used for prison bedding means that it is extremely difficult to tear: The sheets and duvets are purposely made that way, but, these lads are nobodys fool, they are ingenious and resourceful and if they wanted to do or get something, they would strive to find a way of working it out to their advantage.

The burden of enforcing maximised drug control and alleviating the threat of hidden weapons was infinitely apparent to us all. The Governor had drummed it into us, to be vigilant and to ramp up our observation skills; it was imperative, for the safety of every person that walked the landings. We knew we had a tough battle on our hands, however, we also knew that when we all pulled together we would invariably come out on top.

There also appeared to be the deepening issue, where worshippers were starting to exploit their church and prayer times, to distribute some of their illicit contraband. They had started to cause mild distractions during the hour long services and they seemed to think they could get away with passing drugs and tobacco without being detected. Small groups of organised gangs had begun a stealthily growing system. of secreting small packages in some of the most obscure places and then passing on the location of them during their exercise hour. Some of the packages are so minute that they were becoming increasingly hard to notice and were so difficult to detect, they had to be sniffed out by the dogs.

The determination of the prisoners was no less than exceptional, particularly in those who had the misfortune of getting themselves into bad debt. There were many, in depth, time consuming, labour intensive searches required because of it and it only served to put a huge strain on staff. There were numerous extra meetings and a lot of onus was set on implementing sound new measures. A great deal of effort, was put into changing all schedules and an entire revamp of the normal routine was needed, in order to confuse the men involved. The dedicated search team had a proper battle on their hands and it was several weeks before the chain was broken.

Violence reduction intelligence constantly suggested, that there may be an increasing gang culture, which was connected to the rise of drug offences and it was making a marked difference to the whole dynamics of the place. There is a saying, and, it's true, that no-one is for sale but everyone can be bought. Sometimes all it takes to turn a head, is a whispered threat to family and to friends. The versed, systematic and seasoned residents, were often prepared to do whatever it took, to ensure they were going to get what they wanted, against all the odds and at any cost. They are very clever and can often find ways of doing things that even the CCTV and bodyworn cameras will be unable to reveal. Prison officers are certainly not idiots but they are really up against it, twenty four hours a day and seven days a week.

The organization is fraught with danger and you have to really look after yourself, threats abound around every corner and situations can change in a blink of an eye and every minute of the day. You have to have balls of steel and an unflinchable resolve, and, the last thing you want to do is make yourself a target. A reputation as a fair officer, is paramount to getting the tasks done, and as well as gaining respect and trust from your colleagues; everyone has their part to play to ensure the team works together as one. There is simply no other way to get the job done properly. It's a sort of homo-sapien jigsaw puzzle.

Of course there are always the occasional officers who will let themselves down, the industry is such a harsh enviroment to be working in, after all, we are mere mortals and sometimes, individuals can get taken by surprise and be roped in to something before they even know it. The nature of the new recruits, is to please, so they often get overly enthusiastic and try their best to be accommodating. It's not unusual for several of the inmates to attempt to be-friend them, for their own self indulgence and personal or financial gain. However, these incidents are quickly exposed and not much harm is done.

The presence of some regular inmates is undoubtedly likely to cause quite a bit of disruption, sometimes, they choose to stay locked up and totally self-isolate. They are often consumed by self-loathing and can be fiercely aggrophobic. It's very difficult trying to manage these most vulnerable of inmates at the best of times and the ones that refuse to integrate can be the biggest challenge, despite spending all the time in their cells. They can often refuse to come out, unless they feel absolutely safe and it takes specially trained officers to see to their needs and to accompany them if they have reason to leave their units. Some are so afraid to be seen by any of the other prisoners, that they won't even walk down the corridors to shower and some are even too scared to walk past locked units, for fear of being grabbed through the hatches. They tend to edge slowly and purposefully along the walls and refuse to be rushed. It's a tricky test of patience for their Key workers whom, as it happens, do the most amazing job as persoal mentors and their resilience is of real value. They seem to possess an in-built understanding, that, although it might well appear rediculous and bizzare behaviour to outsiders, it's a rare and innate puzzle, that makes sense, only to the brain of the troubled man.

Prescription meds are a hugely valuable commodity and frequently get stolen, they are an easy bargaining tool and the lads are kings of the spin to get them. They are lightening fast as they shoot past each other, to join the line at the meds hatch. The usual excuses are lost on the nurses, they have heard them all before and not many manage to fool them, particularly as they have to swallow them and show an empty mouth before they are allowed to move away. "Come on, Miss, without all my meds I'm just fucked up and I start cutting up!" The repetitive quote falls time after time on selectively deaf ears, as the nurses dutifully refuse to be manipulated into submission, leaving the men less than pleased to be referred back to their doctor.

Some even go to the lengths of vomiting up their swallowed medication, to sell on to the highest bidder. There is nothing that surprises the officers and nothing that the prisoners will stop at if they actually mean business.

Some of the men are little gems. one said he had been told by a good source that his cellmate had a pocket full of bits and bobs that he had nicked from the workshop. He said he heard that he was going to make a tool to cut out a hole in his wall, so that he could pass contraband through to the next cell. When asked who told him this, he replied. "All the voices in my head did!" we thought he was obviously feeding us a load of bullshit, but, every tiny piece of information needs to be soundly checked out, however crazy it may sound. When your life depends on it, you simply don't take any chances.

Sometimes, the most bizzare intelligence will give an unexpected challenge that can cause a big headache and be a total waste of our resources and time, but, other times there is truth in it and lo and behold, there was a hefty make-shift chisel found under the mattress of the bottom bunk. A great deal of damage had already been done. There was a discreet narrow hole that had been chiselled out between the two cells: It was in the far corner behind the bunks and we knew, that all sorts would have already been passed through it, from one prisoner to another. It was not possible to know how long the hole had been in use. This time, the men had almost been too clever for us.

It was time to relocate the key players and put in tight new measures, regarding the follow up intelligence and the hunt for the dispersed contraband. The dog and search teams were called in, and the wing was turned upside down in a matter of a few minutes. The duty Custody Manager was furious and his plain talking was not going down well with one of the inmates, who had been taken out of the workshops for stealing and had already been put on basic regime. He hadn't been involved in the chisel incident but couldnt help mouthing off and telling the officers that they were useless twats. He screamed that if he had to go without his fags or spice again, one of them would be in for it! He obviously knew something, but, it was going to be a long slog finding out exactly what.

"All you lot talk about is false promises, but everyone just tells me what I want to hear, so I wont play up and that's why I want to get spice, it stops me wanting to cut up and I cut up so I can feel real. It makes everything be real again, you can't stop me from cutting up! That therapist is a useless bitch, she just wants to know all my fucking business, so she can tell the Governor and he will get me put back on basic for good. You are bastards, the lot of you are shit. It's your fault I'm like I am!"

He shouted as if his satanic soul had been set free and was about to engage it's final enemy. He lunged forward at the officers, he was brandishing a crudely improvised weapon and screaming obscenities. Each officer new to the scene was next in the firing line and had to take a step back to avoid getting themselves stabbed, or cut. Suddenly he shot between the two officers on the top of the steps and one of them grabbed his arm putting it in a lock behind his back; finally bringing him to his knees and removing the offending weapon from his grasp. It was found to be a piece of a broken plastic spoon that had been sharpened into a point. The crudeness of some improvised weapons are a sign of sheer desperation and it was believed, that on this occasion, the tool was made for his own self defence from his demons. The prisoner obviously needed psychological aid and great care would have to be taken regarding his mental health.

He was quickly restrained and cuffed, but he was totally uncompliant and six of the officers had one hell of a time getting him off the wing, he continued screaming and shouting all the way to the seg.

"Dont think you can fucking fob me off, it's either attack one of you fucking lot, or cut myself up, either fucking way its extra work for you bastards innit! Too late, you fuckers, the stash is gone ha ha, you can stop my TV and canteen; I don't care, my money has already gone into my bank account." The offender was taken to the seg to cool off, the nurse was called and calmness was soon restored to the wing.

Giving the prisoners all the technical and practical skills they need to help them on the outside is a major priority. There are some that really appreciate help and throw themselves into any available opportunity like there's going to be no tomorrow, but, some simply whinge and groan and fling it back in the face of the establishment. We know some will take the skills with them, but, there are all types of characters and all we can do, is help the ones who will accept it and tolerate those who are out to cause chaos.

We never found the contraband that had been dispersed through the narrow hole in the wall but at least a stop had been put to it. Some of the time we feel it's not really a bonus to discover a breach of security that might have already taken place, as the knock on effects can be so devastating and the evidence is gone. However, the upside is, that we can take it on the chin, in the knowledge that quite a significant market has been permanently blocked.

Chapter 4

Whispering Mary

Chapter 4

Whispering Mary

I caught sight of Mary out of the corner of my eye, I think she thought that the more she carried on her belt the more important she looked. The silly cow, she resembled a freaking suicide bomber in drag, it was a miracle that she could get up from her chair draped in all that metal. I hoped she wasn't on the way to the mess, I wanted a quiet cup of tea but I was out of luck, she linked her arm through mine and jangled alongside me to the tea room.

The cups in the sink looked like they had been pissed in and left out in the morning sun to dry. "Dirty bastards, Does no one in this freaking place know where, the hell, the bloody washing up liquid is kept?" Mary angrily grappled with the dishcloth and plastic plates, whilst I boiled the kettle and searched for my biscuits, which had been cruelly plundered along with my bag of cheese and onion crisps and my sugar. We decided to put up a sarcastic notice about the evil act of nicking food that did not belong to you and another about the washing up fairies running away with the tidying up elves.

Poetic licence, however, was to be granted by us, this time and we cleaned the place up, simply because we didn't want to have to sit in a shit hole for rest of our break.

I think it's pretty safe to say, that, the old saying 'What goes on behind closed doors stays behind closed doors, especially the ones with bars on!' Was quite accurate, so I hoped my silly disclosure to Mary stayed with her. She's not a bitch but she barks a lot and I didn't fancy bringing down the wrath of Jeremy upon my head; I hadn't meant to let it slip about his vasectomy, anyway, I was due to be detailed to work with him on the evening shift, so I would soon find out, either way! I carefully practiced my apology and decided to buy him a well deserved pint.

It was the turn of my shift to attend the gym for our annual fitness test and none of us had done much to keep in trim, so, we were all ribbing each other about our shape. "I'm ok, anyway, I've got a good shape, oh, well; I'm round and round is a shape isn't it?" "I bet you haven't seen your bollocks for a year!" "This ass might well be chubby, but, piss off, it's already spoken for!" "Come on; get those chunky butts into your kit, you lazy fat bastards!" "Hey, just because we're here and awake doesn't have to mean we're ready to do anything!" "Exercise doesn't pay the bills, so sod the gym, I'm doing some overtime this afternoon," etc. etc.

The changing rooms are the comedy hub of the place, it's where everyone talks and shares their humour. Insults abounded and the combined bouquet of deodorants and bodily odour permeated the walls. "Your fucking shirt needs to be introduced to an iron!" "Oh, yeah and your big fat fucking stomach should get introduced to some salad!" "The scandalously abusive, highly insulting behavior and mickey-taking was hugely entertaining to say the least and we all joined in, so none of us could complain that we were the only ones being picked on. It was always a battle of the finest wit and sharpest observation.

Ryan started singing and we all threw our shoes at him. We played about a bit more until we finally realized we were running short on time and no one wanted to be late when Senior Officer Lewis was in charge; it wasn't worth the pain. We calmed ourselves down and made our way to the gym in an orderly manner.

I was standing in the training room like a fish, freshly out of safe water, floundering and convinced I was going to fail the test. I kept telling myself that I was in a place where my past wasn't going to define my future and I would get through it, despite eating all those cakes at the weekend. I have to be brutally honest, my legs were most definitely not in tune with my body and it was a struggle. I think I was more afraid of Mr. Lewis than of failing, I knew I had to hang on tight, I knew it was going to be a bumpy ride. I rubbed my flabby calves and wished myself luck.

Senior officer Lewis, held a formidable reputation and I wasn't about to find out if it was true. I heard that his motto, was to face the unexpected and always allow for the unexpected, and believe me, I didn't see his charge coming until he was on me. However, I basked in the applause from the bountiful array of spectators, as I flew through the test in a whirl of fear enduced speed. Lewis, said he knew I had a bit of spunk buried inside me and he slapped my back so hard, that I thought his fist would go through to my chest.

I was significantly out-performed by the other officers but it didn't matter, as I was through and could feel decidedly secure in the knowledge that my job was still safe. I braced myself in readiness for my week of nights that was due to start the following Monday, but, only after I had celebrated over the weekend, of course and until then a cup of tea in the mess would have to do!

I was preoccupied in the tea room, being thoroughly entertained by the admin staff, as they were exceptionally territorial about their personal mugs. It was interesting to watch the rage rising, as a cup was found with the remnants of some tea, or coffee still at the bottom of it. Please stay strong workmates, hey; it's only a bit of dried on drink, you know! It's not the end of the bloody world as we know it!

One of the civvies had her birthday and brought in some cake for everyone. It was like an offering from the Gods. The timing was just perfect and the dirty mugs were soon washed up, re-filled and forgotten all about.

Tom passed me a form to sign, so I asked him if I was his new paperwork bitch and he asked me, if I had bothered to make sure to reinforce the chair I was sitting on! There was much lively banter and we all collapsed with laughter. "He had to grow up too quickly and he's missed out on his childhood, that's why he acts like a kid!" Tom pinged my nipple in response and the excruciating sting of it stopped me in my tracks. "Go and answer those bells you lazy sod, go on, fuck off and do your job! Bloody hell! Are you deaf in both ears, or what?" I didn't mind the banter but the finger flicks really bloody hurt and Tom scarpered away before I had a chance to hit him back.

Lunch break was like feeding time at the zoo, the mess was packed with the hungry officers, ravenously devouring their dry sandwiches and hot soup. It was our down time, our time away from the landings and the constant stress. The silly banter, and craziness was our daily permitted release, and the ribbing was our anxiety buster.

"Has anyone seen my crowbar? I need it to prise those two love-birds apart. They have been arguing for over fifteen years now! "Happy anniversary, anyway, to you guys" Stewart, pointed across the room to Bill and Sue. Just what was missing from my perfect day, was a pair of loved up old fogeys, deriving great pleasure from a public snog: Sue still had her looks but Bill was working very hard to keep up. He most definitely had hair once; however, it probably hadn't flopped across his eyes since the late 80s. They are obviously still loved up and who were we to knock that? It's really nice to see some commitment and I think that quite a few people were probably a bit jealous of their relationship. It can't be easy to work as a husband and wife team in the same place but they had endured the test of time and were both very happy; it was nice, it really was.

The thing about work relationships is that they can catch you unaware: Then before you knew it, you could be launched into a circle of brutally frivolous affairs. Personally, I was inclined to be in preference of keeping my own love life separate from my working life. I wouldn't like to do my bit with someone, after showing my bits to them, then being left out to dry! Most of the married ones are committed to their partners; therefore, it's only going to be a problem if they are that way inclined in the first place!

A subtle eye roll from Clayton, served to show us that break was over and we were needed back on the wings. It was time to end the idle gossip and try to battle the usual, after lunch productivity slump.

"That cake was lovely but I need a drink, it doesn't go down easy, not like you!" Tina winked at me; she just had to slide in one of her cheesy one-liner's, before she sloped off to help out in video link. My call after her, to tell her, that her only best friend was a sausage hand-shake, was lost as the door slammed shut behind her. I'm far too slow with my rebuffs. I need some more practice on them. I wasn't as green as I was cabbage looking but I wasn't very adept at the banter just yet. However, un-deterred, I continued scoffing the birthday cake, then discarded my plate in the sink, along with all the others; the rest room resembled a tornado hit ruin. I scrawled a note saying. "This kitchen was nice and clean yesterday, I'm sorry you missed it!" Then I closed the door on the mess and hoped someone else would do the honours before my next visit.

Chapter 5

Night Lights

Chapter 5

Night lights

Night time patrol can sometimes be really daunting, as some of the inmates play up, knowing there is limited staff on duty and they think it's funny, it's a game to them and they are very good at it. However, it's difficult when there is a real incident and sadly, the night is the time the vulnerable inmates have to be watched like a hawk. It's the time they feel most alone and a time they will tend to do something silly. Luckily, the officers have built up good relationships with most of the men, and they have the knack of keeping them calm and settled. There is also the added bonus of regular intermittent checks, particularly on some of the sensitive individuals that might have shown discontent, and there is always a listener and a nurse to call on if anyone is really unsettled.

The count was done, the numbers in and roll was correct, it was time for everyone to settle themselves down for the night however, some of the lads had other ideas and they started playing their music really loudly, the wing was in uproar. There was screaming and shouting and the air of the entire wing became blue with the most un-mentionable language ever heard.

"Oh for fucks sake, Miss, tell them to shut the fuck up, some of us have got work in the morning!" What the hell, my bloody heart bleeds for you, was the first thought that came to my mind but, they were right, the music was intolerable and the cell-mates refused to stop their partying, it was getting beyond a joke. There were threats of beatings from all around the wing, something had to be done about it and it was down to the Night shift Manager to sort it out. Luckily we had a no-nonsense Officer in charge and the offending radio was quickly confiscated, and the two party animals were moved off to separate cells. Hallelujah!

My comrade for the night sat pouring over the sports news; he had a really bad skin condition which he insisted on picking away at, and his nose had become crispy and was just like the crust of a burnt loaf.

I shouldn't be mean, and after all, he was such a lovely person and is an outstanding officer, but, having a tiger loaf for a nose is the only way to describe how he looked. I did try my hardest not to notice it, but, I didn't manage too well at all.

We did the nightly paper-work, checked that everything on the wing was in order and turned the TV on quietly. Suddenly there was loud crash, as if a door was being smashed in and we ran downstairs to investigate. A blind flapped furiously, like a demented flag, as the wind howled through the bars and caused the sash on the window to twist and tangle. God only knows how the window had come open but it scared the living daylights out of us. It's very weird, how after a scary moment, you are inclined to initiate a debate on whether there are ghosts in the building, or not, and to insist on keeping the lights on for the entire shift.

I had convinced myself that there was a ghoul lurking around somewhere in the building and I found myself stopping for a minute to peek over my shoulder, before heading over to do the checks through the narrow grey openings of the cell doors. I hoped that none of the prisoners would do their silly trick of slowly raising their head from below the gap and into the light from the torch as you shone it in. It never failed to make me jump and was something they found amusing. It was very unnerving and even more so, after listening to the idiotic ghost stories. Luckily, the routine checks went without any incident and I thankfully returned swiftly to the staff room.

We tried to change the subject and started likening some other members of staff to animals, just to pass the time. It was fun at first, but, when the conversations began to get insulting, we thought it was time to put a halt to that too. I mean, it's not really nice to describe someone as a fat slug on speed, or as a neurotic hippo with breath like dog shit, is it? Night time duties can really bring out the worst in you, and sometimes it really needs a bit of reining in. Although, to be quite honest and in our defence, there were indeed several animal similarities to be found and compared, so we genuinely couldn't help ourselves. We all possess our own individual sense of humour and sometimes it can get funnier when it gets misunderstood. We try not to offend, however, it goes with the territory and our shoulders are broad enough to take it.

At 4 a.m when you are bored to death and the wing is quiet, you can't help slipping back into your evil debauchery and start to say things like; "Don't you think Mr. Parker has an uncanny resemblance to Mr. Burns from the Simpsons?" Or, "What do you think of that skinny twat, Williams, sporting his new handlebar tash?" "Hey, Wolverine was on good form yesterday and hasn't the Thunder-cat shown his true colours today." "Did you know that Darth Vader, has got himself a new puppy?" etc.

Crispy nose, called me a spiteful cow and shuffled off downstairs to do some work on the computer; so, I had a quick scoot around and watched some rubbish telly in between checks, until the morning cover arrived for the handover. Anyway, having to look at tiger nose kept making me want to make myself a sandwich. I was glad he had gone off downstairs, to the office and out of the way, as he was making me feel really hungry, and sick at the same time.

I enjoyed working the nights, especially if you were on with a good crowd of staff. The time passed by quickly if everyone pulled their weight and shared out the load, and the banter was second to none most of the time. It can feel a bit daunting being locked inside, but it's good to know you always have back up: However harsh the banter becomes, the commitment to each other is still sound.

There will always be the odd exception, of course, particularly when you really think you have seen a ghost and you get scared, and your annoying workmates insist on sharing a scary story, or two, just before it's your turn on the rounds. I swear that one night I sensed a presence on the dark stairs leading down from the top landing of B Wing, but, when I told the others, they insisted on taking the proverbial and maintained it was where an old officer walked and jangled his keys as a warning.

They told me he would brush across my face with his hand, if I went a bit too near the arched window. They stated that the same ghost had already appeared twice before, to a young officer and she had not been able to work nights after that, as she was too afraid of seeing him again.

I tried not to take any notice; however, I must admit, that I had a shiver each time I had to walk the landing, on my own and in the pitch dark, with only a torch and radio to keep me company.

I was glad to be off the main wings for the remainder of the time, as, after seven full nights of horror stories, I was beginning to suffer from severe stress and anxiety my-self. Thank goodness for the mental health policy that has been put in place to serve the staff. My God, working nights with Stan was like frying my bloody pet rabbit. On the one hand, he could charm all the monkeys out of their trees to chop their balls off and on the other hand he was like a wild animal released. I had never, ever, worked with anyone like him before and it had been a very strange encounter, he was hilariously funny but he was also utterly exhausting.

After the week of night shifts, I was glad to look forward to some time with Mum, she had promised to join me for a walk on the beach and a trip into town, to get some new skinny jeans. I wasn't really holding my breath about it, and I assumed I would probably end up having to make do, with the usual couple of nights snuggled up on the settee, watching her favourite films and devouring copious bottles of red wine, but, I didn't mind at all, as long as she was happy! My Mother is my hero and I am always happy if my Mum is happy.

I found myself thinking out loud, perhaps I really should make a bit of a better effort to find myself a cool boyfriend, to spend some time with. I was sure Mum would love to be involved with me planning my wedding; it would really give her some-thing positive to focus on.

I needed someone who would bring out the hidden Cinderella in me. I wasn't very good at dating, the few times I had tried it,

I was left feeling awkward and ugly and the men I met were usually only interested in the apparatus I have between my legs. Unfortunately for them, my vagina is only available to those by personal invitation and I wasn't willing to compromise, what the hell was I? Rent A Vag or something? I secretly wished for someone; to please go out with me, without having an ulterior motive. Or at least give me time to brush the cobwebs away before suggesting any recreational gymnastics in the bedroom.

Some of the men I met could be incredibly sexist and the trouble was that they didn't even realize they were offensive. Others appeared void of any personality but some were cutely nerdy. I just couldn't seem to hit upon the right balance and in any case, I was getting fed up of hanging around with total strangers and talking rubbish for hours on end; on topics I knew nothing at all about. Although with due respect, I had enjoyed a fair few free dinners.

Chapter 6

Inspiration

Chapter 6

Inspiration

The bald Casanova smiled and winked as he skilfully maneuvered his lorry into the vehicle lock area. The idiot is such a gimp warrior; he loves being searched by the female officers and never fails to give a stupid or sarcastic, and sometimes a sexist comment. I'd love to take his half baked French sticks and shove them up his fat saggy arse. I know, it's a cruel sentiment but I can't help myself. You know how it is, when you see a certain person and all you immediately want to do, is pull each eyelash out, as slowly and as painfully as possible. Tugging on them, one at a time and simply enjoying the vision of their stretched lids popping.

The only thing in life that's constant, is change and I wished baldy would change; he seemed to believe he was so amusing but his jokes were lost on me! "I think all men should be married eh, none of us daft buggers should be allowed to be happy!" "If you say so but could you please rein in the jokes, as I'm really busy today and we need to get the yard cleared quickly!" "Oh someone got out of the wrong side of the bed this morning, if you were in my bed you wouldn't want to get out at all!" I sometimes felt a bit sorry for him, as he smacked of loneliness, but, he was such a sleaze and his bad breath almost made me faint. "Hey come on, pack it in, Casanova, let's hurry up and get these food crates sorted!" Was my altogether pitiful reply!

It's at moments like this you learn what it is you are made of and I know what I'm made of, it's jelly. I just wobble and hope to stay standing. I wished I had the wit and clever banter of my peers, but, I was nowhere near as quick witted as they were and I was invariably slow with my retorts. Sometimes, when I was caught up in the middle of a ribbing session, I would find myself slightly bricking it. I was very easy pickings out there, as I took it on the chin, but I didn't often hit back as effectively as I should have, and so, I was generally left howling like a bad ass dog. Of course, everyone else thinks it's funny but my skin is thick and both shoulders are broad and I truly believe that they wouldn't do it to me, if it really upset me, because, after all, if your peers are ribbing you to your actual face, then it means you are now an accepted part of the team and you should be grateful for it! But some are not, and are quick to report you.

In a perfect world, we would all succeed in a civilized manner: In our line of work, we are lucky enough to be surrounded by like-minded people; they get our sense of humour and we also get theirs and it's in everyone's interest to try to get along. Of course, there are times when a personality clash will become apparent and it stands to reason that not everyone will hit it off, as perhaps they should and it's extremely rare to be disliked by everyone. Although, there can always be that one exception to the rule. You have to be clear, about what it is about them, that drives you nuts and then you can create a boundary that will keep you sane if you have to work with them. I usually tried to imagine that they couldn't really have helped becoming so obnoxious because they had endured such a hard life, then I started to feel sorry for them instead and it made our joint tasks easier to manage. It didn't happen often, as most of us in the group get on really well with each other, and a good rapport is the norm. However, it goes without saying of course, there is always one exception and ours was Arabella!

God only knows, what her motives were at that precise moment in time, however; Arabella seemed to be up to her old tricks again. I'm convinced she has a broomstick safely parked up somewhere nearby.

Of course, you shouldn't have to put up with anything you may feel uncomfortable with, but, Arabella, didn't put up with a single thing, from anyone, at any level, however small or insignificant it may be; well, not without making a formal written complaint to one of the Governors.

No one expects anything from her unless it's for her own gain, of course, but, when you become afraid to speak out for fear of retribution, it can get a little bit difficult to function properly. You constantly have to watch your back but you shouldn't have to watch it from a colleague. She's not one of the individuals who can inspire people around her the most, as it was not in her nature to be kind or understanding.

Apparently, she openly describes herself as damaged goods, following her hideous marriage and she hates all men as a result.

Arabella's, ex-husband had been a junior governor at a women's prison and he had been caught sleeping with an inmate. It's a very rare thing, but, it happened and after the fallout, she spent months totally out of it on Prozac and copious bottles of red wine. She didn't manage to cope too well and had been transferred here to Scupton.

She hadn't really endeared herself on the first day, when she called us all a bunch of whining fannies and shouted at us to get a life and to snap the shit out of it. Then she put in a formal complaint regarding our total incompetence: she accused the group of putting her safety at risk, by failing to establish and relate to her, that one of the prisoners may be a threat to females. It was a simple fact she could quite easily have gleaned herself, by reading his files and checking the red card in his door slot. She was difficult to communicate with, at the best of times and Officer Rose took her to one side, to check if she was ok and see if she was perhaps dyslexic. It was done discreetly and with good intentions, as Arabella had quite often misunderstood written instructions. He was really nice and offered her some help and support, but, that afternoon, she reported him to the senior manager, for bullying and making her feel like a fool in front of the other officers!

It appeared that all she wanted to do, was to make waves and see people take a fall, and, however hard we tried to include her in the team, she simply refused our offers of friendship: She really carried the most unusual characteristics, but, I suppose, for some people, offering support is pointing out their weaknesses and confirming their shortfalls, and it can, perhaps come across as a little bit insulting. We simply did not know what to do, to instigate making her warm towards any of us, and, Arabella, was adamant that she was not going to let us inside her mind. It was a constant battle of wits and a daily trial and we all lived in the hope that she would settle down and find harmony with us at some point. We always invited her to join in with us if we were doing anything socially, however, she always told us to get lost. She spent most of her time at work, shouting at us to get out of her fucking way and criticizing our management of tasks. She could not see any other way except hers and she was not always right. The loudest argument is not necessarily the winning one.

We knew our limitations and nothing we could do would shut the woman up. There was nothing to hold her back, it seemed that, whatever happened, it was invariably her move and her genius was apparent.

Above all, she knew many people in the hierarchy: For some reason her side of the stories were always believed, despite any evidence to the contrary, so it came to the point, that the complaints kept rolling in and our arses kept getting kicked. I had never worked with anyone like her before; however, she was an unvarying source of entertainment for us as there was always a trivial issue being discussed.

We were constantly on deputy Governor alert, but, quite frankly as the quote goes, we didn't give a damn. Bollocks to it all, there was nothing with any substance to it, it was all just trivial nonsense and there was nothing tangible in her complaints. She continued behaving like a bitter and scorned woman; spectacularly causing as much upset and torment as possible, for those around her and we learned to live with it; in the hope that she would maybe discover somewhere different to work her wickedness, but, until that day we counted on Karma to kick her arse. Sadly, that day came sooner than we expected.

"She's not running because she's innocent is she? Psycho mare had no sense to stop and she went all out for it, she's lost the plot!" The accusations swiftly circulated. A crazy incident, is how it was described, Arabella, said she couldn't have done it as she would never have let herself become so irresponsible. She cried and howled like a scalded cat when the police came to arrest her. She begged for a psychiatrist to diagnose her deeply seated anxiety issues. She insisted that she suffered from PTSD and condemned everyone around her for failing to support her in her time of need.

How difficult it can be, to help the people who refused to help themselves! It was a marked learning curve for us, as a team. We were shocked and upset that we had not noticed the signs of imminent danger. We had never failed to notice them in the prisoners, but, we had missed them in one of our own: We had, somehow, allowed ourselves to become a little bit complacent due to Arabella's insolence, her constantly erratic behaviour and unfriendly attitude towards us had been dismissed as plain rudeness. We tried hard with her but I suppose in the end we simply gave up.

Arabella, had taken one of the new young officers, from B wing; she had him in an arm-lock and marched him into a cell, she struck him hard with her baton and his head was bleeding, he had fallen to the floor and she kicked him until he cried for mercy. She barricaded the door, so, we couldn't get inside and she screamed at anyone who tried to get near. We tried to reason with her but she was beyond all reasonable logic.

Eventually, she came out of the cell and made a run for it towards the main gate. Apparently, the boy looked like her ex. She insisted that he had been flirting and suggestive and she had seen red when he tried to give her a little kiss. It had been a bizarre day but it was a little bit calmer now, it was such a shame that she hadn't shared her pain with us, instead of losing control. We had all tried our very best to welcome her, at first, but, she had seemed intent on alienating us and it made us sad it had come to this end.

Keeping safe comes at a very high price, for the officers and prisoners alike. Every person, at whatever level, is expected to play their part, safely and responsibly and integrity is paramount. It's very difficult to establish the mutual trust that keeps emotions and actions contained, as it can only take a single instant for everything to fall apart, we have to be constantly aware of everything and everyone around us and each new day will inevitably bring forward new challenges and passions.

No-one really wanted to cause any unnecessary trouble; not even the cheekiest inmates. It was better to get the day done and dusted without incident, it was better for everyone's sake and luckily, the only other problem that day, was some of the prisoners fooling around and dropping their towels and shirts over the stairwells and on to the heads of the officers below; plus a little disagreement about some bars of soap and a few missing choccy bars.

Some people are simply best left alone, as they will always remain a stranger and no amount of reassurance or encouragement will ever inspire them to engage with you, or to identify with you. If only she could have felt more confident to be honest with us about her mental health issues, instead of shutting us out. We knew there was a problem but we just couldn't find a way inside Arabella's head, as she was too far gone in her private despair. Her story was far from over, as for her, it was just the beginning, of an all embracing, long term healing process and despite her behaviour, we all wished her well!

Chapter 7

Affairs Of The Heart

Chapter 7

Affairs Of The Heart

I have to admit, that for the main part, the staff are absolutely wonderful, however, the place also has it's fair share of the most utterly bizzare human beings, too. I think the diversity is probably the prison's best kept secret. It has often crossed my mind, that maybe, some of the poor souls must endure such an absurdly raw deal outside the workplace, that they feel they have to re-invent themselves in work. The result being, that even their physicalities and feelings become utterly transformed, as they enter the gateway of the establishment to start a brand new day.

I had noticed that some of them were quite shockingly un-original during their metamorphosis, but, some became outrageous and comical beyond all reason and I was inwardly amused by it all.

I was constantly entertained by the quirky individuals compelled to place themselves outside their very own comfort zones, for the sake of being noticed and the fear of being exposed as a fraud.

As I approached the smoking area, I heard voices. "You convinced yourself that you love me! No, I never said I loved you, we just used each other for some comfort, I told you that I couldn't commit to you." I didn't mean to overhear the conversation but I couldn't help it and once it had been heard it couldn't be unheard. I knew Jenny must be feeling like crap, she had been warned about Brad. His bad reputation preceded him and everyone knew he was married, but, he had managed to claw her in, somehow; and now he was letting her down and not gently. I silently sneaked away and decided I would find Jenny later to check how she was. I wouldn't let her know I had been behind the wall, on my ciggie break and had heard every word. I think that would only serve to embarrass her and I didn't want to upset her any more than she obviously would be, after that conversation.

I know it's wrong to tar everyone with the same brush, so to speak, but, bloody men, some of them just couldn't keep it in their boxers! for God's sake, didn't the girl see any of the signs of disaster. The truth was, there was a fresh influx of new recruits on the horizon and it appeared that our Brad, amongst others, was on the lookout for leaner meat. Bloody horrible bastard, he's a conniving twat and I can't help feeling sorry for his wife, if only she knew what he was really like.

I detest betrayal, it's a really destructive monster, particularly in a big place full of ugly whispers, like this.

Shame of it was, that Jenny's husband had left her and Brad had honed in when she was in a sad and dark place and was very vulnerable. I think she thought that being shown attention proved to her that she was still an attractive and desirable woman in her own right and it had flattered her.

Of course, it's no one else's concern and they are consenting adults at the end of the day, however, she had simply disregarded Brad's terrible reputation and had gone against the advice of everyone around her.

Perhaps reckless behaviour, is an excuse to dull the pain of heart-break and no one could possibly know the things Brad had promised her and anyway, whatever it was it wasn't on the cards now.

By the way, Officer Jenny Latimer, is in fact, absolutely gorgeous and could easily have anyone she wanted, but, I think this blow is going to mess up her confidence for a while and I could batter Brad's head for doing that to her.

Of course, shit happens, I know it, but, in this place, every day is a neverending shit storm. Best I organise a girly night pretty soon, one with plenty of wine and tissues. At least Jen's vagina had had a bit of fun, all mine did was ovulate, pee and bleed.

Everyone appeared, on the surface, to be outraged by Brad's insensitive behaviour and gave Jenny loads of the support she deserved, but, of course there was going to be the inevitable, degeneratively cruel banter at her expense. The worst mainly coming from the direction of the usual heartless mutton heads, who deserved no naming, as we all knew who they were. It was to be expected; if we are truly honest, however, most of the fellow officers were sympathetic and very supportive in reality.

Anyway, I managed to organize my girlie wine night with Jen and it turned out she was positively devastated and she insisted that he was actually a good guy, once you got to know him; although she did admit that she knew that it wasn't going to last. After several hours of talking, it seemed that the penny had finally dropped, and in the end, she cried, she laughed and she screamed, but, despite her sadness; for the most part we managed to laugh. She tried to explain that having sex had been her only way to communicate, as she wanted to find a way to actually feel something, without having to talk. I suppose I did sort of understand what she meant, but I didn't ask her to embellish, I just gave her more wine and hugs. I think the wine helped a lot but our heads paid a high price for it the next day.

The following morning, Jen and I joined the officers doing the long walk towards the high grey walls. A discernible figure hovered in the window above the main gate and we all knew it was the Governor, scanning the troops as we piled in through the heavy secure doors to collect our keys.

Our Governor, commanded the greatest of respect and he bloody well got it. He was physically small but his personality made up for his size. It was a sort of love hate relationship with most of us, he was fair, but harsh if you got on the wrong side of him, and, woe betide you if he caught you taking the piss. I actually quite liked him but there again, I had never done anything to annoy him as far as I know and I simply kept my head down and did what I needed to do: I completed all my tasks on time and kept out of his way, as I didn't fancy my head exploding from one of his rants. I didn't think I could bear it, definitely not with a hangover anyway.

"Trouble brewing then?" Officer Jackson pointed to the figure behind the glass, then did a dead punch to my arm. I hated it so much when he did that, he thought it was funny, but I fucking well didn't. It bloody well hurt like holy hell, but, the more I objected to it, the harder he did it, so I just ignored it for fear of more pain.

The morning briefing was buzzing for the second time that month. All the night staff had been kept back to attend it, and the Governor had been in since four a.m. He stood before the attentive gathering and although he appeared controlled and calm, you could sense the underlying fury.

I managed to make some eye contact with Officer Townsend, I knew she had worked through the previous night shift, and she looked pretty shaken up. I sat with her and asked what had happened. "Oh my God, Parsons, up on A wing, got attacked with a hard plastic shank, for God's sake, it just missed his airways and his jugular but has caught an artery. What a freaking mess, poor bastard resembled a fucking smashed jam jar on the floor, he is lucky to be still alive!"

"A fucking home-made knife, sliced right through his neck, for fucks sake, Sheridan did it, the evil bastard, he meant to do him some real harm, he must have been really frightened." There was abundant free for all speculation and unbridled discussion, mainly regarding the heinous debt the men allow themselves to accrue. Hundreds of pounds that they can ill-afford, simply to acquire the meaningless bit of splif, for their only pleasure, and their escape into temporary oblivion from the drudgery of their daily lives. A world where they lived in fear of becoming broken down, by the impending boredom and inactivity.

The staff try to reason with the prisoners, but, there are some things that cannot be explained or taught. The awful events of the previous night was a major worry. The home made weapon had been concealed somewhere really well, so much so, that the officers hadn't noticed it, and it was absolutely apparent that the knife could have easily been used on one of the staff, if that had been the intention. The gravity of the situation was indisputable.

The improvised shank made from a plastic plate was a definitive piece of evidence, it had been corroborated and safely stored in an evidence bag. It was imperative that no further weapons were secreted anywhere else and the search teams and the dogs were already hard at work. The situation was well under control and the prisoner at the centre of the disruption, had been duly arrested and was being interviewed by the police down the isolation unit. The victim had been taken to intensive care and the family liaison team were with his next of kin. We hoped the situation would not turn into a murder investigation and we prayed that common sense would prevail on the wings. The Governor had the sole responsibility for the safety of each and every individual in his establishment, and that safety had been duly threatened.

The Number one, wanted the answers and he was damned well going to get them and get them quickly. His staunch reputation was on the line and he had no intention of losing face. We stood assured that the bad situation would be dealt with immediately and without fail, as we knew the Governor would up the anti. There was no doubt that he would get to the bottom of it and he had our utmost support.

We knew we could depend on him, he had shown time and time again, that he was in our corner and we were blanketed in his trust. It was true, that our Governor had had his fair share of knocks, both on and off the battle-fields. He had commenced his prison career as an operational support grade and assisted the officers with their daily tasks, and he had committed his life to the service.

He was soon discovered to be a frugally honest and reliable individual and had worked his way up through the ranks with gusto and determination, earning respect wherever he was posted. He had fought his way through diversity and inequality. He was intelligent and nobody's fool. He knew all the tricks in the book of life. He had been up against it himself, many times and had come through and now he was back with such a vengance in his later life, that he really was some mega force to be reckoned with: Our Number one Governor was not really well known for his cuddly nature, however, he had our backs and for that we were grateful.

Chapter 8

My First Dressing Down

Chapter 8

My First Dressing Down

"Are you in a different fucking universe? I'm no expert, but, that's a freaking stupid and naïve attitude, what the fuck are you doing working in a place like this if that's how you feel? You can't let your bloody guard down for a single minute, or they will have you! Best you piss off now and work on someone else's shift, you dopey cow! I'll be fucked if I'm having you to back me up; you'd better call in a fucking favor and swap your detail!" That's the trouble with this place, now, they pay you less and they get people like you coming here and thinking you are going to fix the bloody world. Fucking monkeys the lot of you, bloody new ones, go and find another job, somewhere else. I don't know where though, perhaps you can find a place they can appreciate your ridiculous bloody do-gooding fucking nonsense!"

Oh my God! This was my first experience of Officer George, he was as wild as hell and didn't pull his punches, he scared the shit out of me, but, I stood steadfast in his rage. Bloody hell, I was sure I felt a little bit of wee escape but luckily, I'm a very big panty liner fan so there's not too much harm done. I glanced around the room and silently thanked the others for supporting me. Bunch of two faced bloody wankers; every single one of them, had previously been belly-aching about Officer George, but, they all just sat and watched me being destroyed. Perhaps I am a stupid monkey, so, perhaps I should piss off from here and find somewhere monkeys will be made more than welcome, but why should I go? After all who wants to be paid in peanuts eh?

I thought the reprimand was rather harsh for the first offence of a green-gilled new recruit. My crime being, only, that I had given a book to one of the prisoners to give to his cellmate and I shouldn't have. I had made a mistake and I understand that now, but, surely he could have simply taken me to one side and explained, that the answer to the prisoners' should always be no, whatever the question. He really was making an example of me. Anyway, it was one of the other officers had asked me to do it, for them, but, I was not going to let on to Officer George about that. So I just apologized profusely and took it on the chin. I prayed it was a power seeking ploy, for him to show his superiority, then he might leave me alone in the future. Anyway, I was sure I would live to fight another day, damp knickers or not.

Officer Sid George, however, was still off on one, he seemed to have absolutely no volume control and my ears began to hurt so much, I was afraid they might start to bleed. I decided it was about time for a toilet break and although I was a jellified mass inside, I tried not to show it, as I excused myself and dragged my sorry arse to the rest-room, with the booming voice of the angry senior officer resounding in my throbbing ears. What the fuck, who the hell did he think he was and did he never bloody shut the hell up? I decided I was simply going to ignore him.

"There are all sorts in here, some have the power of good, but, a lot of these fuckers have the powers of evil and believe me, they are all looking for recruits." He was right of course, it could have been the first stages of corruption and I knew that some of the most unique and incredible minds, worked diligently behind the cold metal doors that securely detained them. Their acute intelligence never failed to astound me and I felt a profound despondency that those resourceful brains were not used for other, more worthwhile purposes, rather than working so vigorously at ducking and diving and bringing themselves into this place.

"He thinks he is invincible, he thinks he is the king of the world, take no notice, his tongue will be lashing at someone else's confidence tomorrow, you know, he just can't seem to help himself, he's such a dickhead and he likes to scare the crap out of all the new ones." Officer Sally Mason stood outside the loos as I came out. I lied and told her that I wasn't really bothered about him and his disgusting temper and he should grow up. Sally put her arms around my shoulders, but, I wasn't really comforted, as I knew that she would go silent as soon as we re-entered the board room. I was right: Sally sat at the opposite end of the big room, Officer George eye-balled me as if to intimidate me again. I politely smiled at him and took the seat nearest the door. It appeared that bullying was being condoned by everyone present and I wondered what the Governor would think about all that. I thought Perhaps I should go and inconvenience him with a quiet little visit! I looked around at my peers and it dawned on me, that in their eyes, I was simply wading through the puddles and learning how to take it in my stride and fight my own battles.

I decided against the visit to the Governor, but, I knew that evening would consist of my own sorry company, a large gin and tonic and a bit of quiet desperation and wailing. The incident had upset me and as I prayed for home time to come quickly, I secretly harboured the idea of making a pact with the devil

Still reeling from my verbal thrashing, I made my way over to the main yard where some officers were having trouble getting the men from D wing back into their cells after exercise. The situation was getting a bit loud. "Hey boss, give us a bit of slack, its ok for you innit, you can go home at the end of the day, we are stuck in here!" Officer Simmonds, was his usual quick witted self, with his reply of, "Yes but you lot have it easy in here, have you seem my wife, I've got to go back home to that ugly fucker!" The lads laughed and the mood lightened as they made their way across the exercise yard and back to their cells. I settled down for the remainder of the shift and thought the job was not so bad after all, especially with officers like Simmonds around to cheer everyone up.

Chapter 9

A Cheap Little Mystery

Chapter 9

A Cheap Little Mystery

Bigger fish than him had tried to reduce me to tears in the past and I was not about to be intimidated by anyone. I tried my best to keep holding on to the door but my strength was undoubtedly lacking to that of his, and as the handle slipped through my hands, the huge grin changed into the familiar sneer. He said I was an economist and that we were all economists in here, especially with the truth and no one would believe the word of a new recruit over a well established officer. I lashed out with my boot and my aim was spot on, as he collapsed to the hard floor clutching his balls. "You can't hide away forever, you little slag!" rang in my ears as I scarpered to the cafeteria.

Several eyes were on me as I threw myself on to the nearest chair, everyone wanted to know what the matter was but I told them I fell on the stairs. I didn't want to have to say what had really happened, as who knows what they would conjure up and I wasn't in the mood for any banter. I wished I had a loyal boyfriend that I could go home and cry to, and then, perhaps he would go and beat him up for me.

Everyone has their own life's story and although you might think that you can't change yours, you actually can; well, the ones ahead of you anyway, and, believe me, I was on track to change the tale of Officer West and his harassment. I just didn't quite know how to go about it yet, as there had been no witnesses. I decided it was now time for people to know how things really were with him, but, I would bide my time and let him drop himself in it, unless I happened to kill him first!

The general alarm jolted me away from my murderous thoughts and we all raced with gusto towards the incident. One of the men had thrown a powerful punch at another prisoner for stealing his vape. He had missed his target and hit one of the others instead, which had resulted in a free for all and there were now five lads laying into him. The situation was swiftly under control but the main instigator was having a panic attack and was thrashing around on the floor, he was fitting and had some foam coming from his mouth. The nurse arrived on the scene and gave him a shot and he was soon sitting down quietly, on his bunk. He was shaken and pale and had started to cry into his pillow.

Officer Shackford adopted her customary soft tones and managed to calm him down almost immediately. She was a tiny little person but she was strong and resilient, her size belied her tenacity and she simply had the enviable knack of comforting, if there is such a thing. She gently patted his arm and told him it was ok to cry when things get too much for you, as even the clouds start to cry when they get a bit too heavy. I wished I had just a smidgeon of her diplomacy, she was such a natural and everyone adored her, even down to the most hardened inmate. Yes, if any of us could pacify the situation with sobriety, it was her. Everyone stood back and allowed Penny Shackford to work her magic and before we knew it, the gibbering wreck before us had been transformed and was apologizing for being responsible for the incident. OK, I will freely admit that I was highly jealous of her skills at diplomacy, but overtly grateful she was on our team. The nurse checked on the prisoner after a while and he said he couldn't remember a thing. He was put on a regular watch for twenty four hours as a precaution.

The men were exhilarated by the incident and started with their nonsense. "Come on now, Miss, show us a little bit of slip and slide!" I wasn't having any of it, they try it on constantly, but, I knew what they were up to. They say you will get wiser with age but that seems to be another thing they fucked up, as they keep coming in and out of jail all the time, it's almost a way of life for them, I say almost; although it may actually be a fact. Throughout my limited time served, I've seen three generations from the same family coming and going. No matter how much help they receive inside these walls, there's nothing on the outside to keep them there. In all fairness though, where else are they going to get a warm bed and food in their stomach? In the strangest of ways, they look on prison as their home, a place they can be safe and free from the horrors of street life, so, despite their pleas of, "I'm on the other side of it now:" and "I'm going to get myself sorted out, so I can be happy:" or "You won't see me in here again Miss!" we usually assumed they were just empty statements, as for some of the men, it's all they know.

I can't believe I used to listen to all their shit with a straight face, I've realised that if you pay attention to the person you are dealing with, you can often see that he is winging it. They think they are cleverer than us but we are taught what to look for, and how to report suspicious behaviour. A lot of them are just like forgotten children, but, under their façade there is a beating heart that circulates their lifes blood just the same as in anyone else. However, the issues like a lack of trust, naiveity and peer pressure, will constantly deliver them back to a life inside these imposing walls.

Sometimes there is simply no hope, as for many of the men, it's the only life they have known. In an odd way, trust is not for sale, but it can easily be bought and sold on the outside, and the hardest of the men could often become entrapped, in a downward spiral. I was quickly learning to read them, with the sound help of my peers and was not overly shocked to see them come back inside.

The diligence of my fellow officers never ceased to impress me. I hoped I would be up to the job, and I would eventually find myself less in awe of them and more in tune with their shrewd intelligence.

I had yet to decide my hand where our delightful Officer West was concerned. His behavior had quickly become a cause for concern, not just to me but to a large number of the other female staff. There had been some serious complaints coming forward and just like me, at first, everyone had thought he was just being a bit of a chauvinistic twat; you know, the type of idiot that assumes that because he has a penis, he should be in charge. However, it had stepped up a scale and he was starting to make quite a lot of the female officers feel very uncomfortable. It was only going to be a matter of time before the shit hit the fan, in that department; it was already a foregone conclusion. So I secretly hoped that the sexist idiot, would refrain from joining us at the party on the weekend, as I didn't want to spend my evening, hiding from his wandering hands and suggestive comments.

Chapter 10

Just A Bit Of R & R

Chapter 10

Just A Bit Of R & R

The entertainment was random, to say the least, really, I mean, the balloon man, for Gods' sake. I actually thought it was quite an incredibly bizzare thing to have at a prison officers works party: I had been expecting something perhaps a little more intriguing, like a good old rock band or a disco and photobooth, or some such thing. It was down to us for being lazy bastards and letting someone like Ollie organize it, just because we couldn't be bothered! At least he tried, even if he was an idiot and after we had called him a serial wanker, we were lucky to have anything at all. We couldn't imagine how dull it would have been if we hadn't invited Terry? He was always the joker in the pack, you know, the funny one, that easily gets everyone laughing out loud, and will invariably be the first one up to sing on the karaoke. Terry was constantly flirting with failure and kissing the bottom of the beer glass, he drinks far too much, but no one has ever pointed it out, the trouble is that he uses the C word far too much, and it's so easy to get into a big fight, as quite a lot of people take exception to that expression.

Steph and I, eyed up the buffet table that resembled a kid's tea party, the choc chip cupcakes were certainly not going to be the right thing to compliment the cider, lager and jager bombs. Anyway, beggars can't be choosers; and it was down to us for not stepping up to the mark in the first place and contributing something towards it. The food wasn't up to much but at least there was something to eat, and anything was better than nothing, to soak up the copious amounts of alcohol this lot would consume. It was destined to be a feast to remember but for all the wrong reasons!

"They say life begins at 40, so, im hoping it's true!" Clive Langford, the birthday boy, himself, bounced in and was first at the bar, closely followed by Flaky, hoping for his freebees as usual. The cocky tight fisted bastard. He knew there would be the predicted tab behind the bar and he was determined, as always, not to miss out. The room soon started to fill up and loud banter could be heard as tables and chairs were being dragged around. "You need a real man to help you do that!" "Well if you can find one mate, that will be great!" "Fuck me, I wanted pasties and sarnies not fucking jelly and ice cream!" "Bloody hell just look at that buffet, where the fuck is the Mad Hatter?"

The room quickly became crammed with workmates and the most insanely comical, intelligent and interesting conversations began to flow, I must say, I am astounded by the effortless and clever wit of all my colleagues, and I can only speak from my heart, when I say, that these officers knew how to work hard and they knew even better how to party hard. I appreciate it sounds like a bit of a cliché, but, I really was proud to be a part of the team. I had found something I loved doing and people I loved spending time with.

The dancing was less of a case of can-can and more like cant-cant!! It was hilarious. We all had an absolute ball, as usual, and although we had maliciously mocked the buffet offering, it hadn't stopped us from demolishing it like ravenous hyenas. Far too much alcohol was guzzled and it was one of my greatest accomplishments, to date, to have managed to stay up on both feet, until well after midnight and not have been sick all over my shoes.

Of course, it goes to say, that not many of our staff nights out, go without incident and Clives' 40th was no exception. The bloody idiot couldn't keep his hands to himself and accusations were soon flying in every direction. "You fucking arsehole, get your filthy hands off me, what the hell!" Rusty managed to step in between Clive and the beast rolling up his sleeves, as he loomed towards him. "She spilled her drink and I was just wiping it down!"

Clive raised his hands up in his defence, "Sorry mate a total misunderstanding, you lucky bastard she's a looker, here, let me get you a round in." It had been a head injury waiting to happen, as we are well aware how quickly things can turn ugly. Needless to say, we were relieved when he was pulled into a handshake and the most it cost him was a pint of guinness and a large pink gin. We all know that if the shit hits the fan you have to take the spray and we all stand together, whether at work or outside.

Not that I'm looking to make an example out of anyone in particular, but, a certain someone is proving to be a problem with staff nights out, as, inevitably there will always be that one pissed up dickhead that wants to fight the world! And he can't resist them.

I must say that the officers had turned out looking very dapper and smart, some, in highly fashionable gear, that really suited them and the girls looked bloody amazing in their glamorous civvies. Their uniforms tend to hide a nice figure and a majority of them were most definitely fit. With their boring, black and whites, no longer hiding their beauty and their hair tumbling down, it was a sight to behold!

"Come on guys, throw all your mobiles on the table and whoever has their wife ring up first, has to get a round in!" Carly was already intoxicated, in fact she had arrived sloshed and her boobies had developed a mind of their very own, and were already hanging out of her tight playsuit, or dress with legs as the lads had described it. She struggled to keep them contained, but, her oversized bangers had other ideas: Apart from trying our best to avoid huge breasts swinging dangerously close to our drinks and trying to ignore the buttons screaming for help, we managed to get on with the dancing and started to relax and have a bit of awesome and well deserved fun. When you put yourself in danger every day, it's only natural that you party as if there is no tomorrow.

We were largely entertained by Vanessa, she had been flirting relentlessly with a hunky barman: She is very attractive and by all means, if you've got it, flaunt it: He eventually asked her to dance but she said he was a bit creepy, she said she had felt his gentleman area touching her stomach, when he pulled her closer to him and it had turned her off.

There is something rewarding about a fun night out, it gratifies your soul and makes you feel that life is worthwhile. I try not to put too many expectations on having a crazy, wild time, as quite often, the best laid plans can just fade into oblivion, and the nights that can turn out to be the most fun, are usually the unplanned and random ones. Or the nights like this, where we were all loosening up and letting the night take us wherever it was going to go. Isn't it odd, that the people who said they would join us for just one quick drink, to be sociable and then leave, were the very ones that started suggesting double shots and then would end up friend-bitching in the toilets, between bouts of vomiting, or walking the streets, in bare feet, all giggly and half dressed.

The evening was once again interrupted by some jumped up little upstarts. They had recognized one of the officers from court and decided they were going to have a go. It was too late to stop them, as they were already wading in like there was no tomorrow, and I hoped they knew what they were doing, as our lot would take no prisoners, if you please pardon the pun. There was a fracas and we were all thrown out but not before Gold, Silver and Bronze was won by our lads. The local idiots had no chance and they were either very brave or stupid, to have even tried it on in the first place. Prison officers are just like the musketeers, all for one and one for all. They are resolute and had no need to justify their existence.

I was slightly terrified, but, the night had been amazing and we had been having a really good time until the fight: We happy footed it to the next bar along and carried on regardless. Luckily, there were to be no further incidents, and we all managed to salvage the remainder of the night. I tried to limit my alcohol intake, as I already knew I was detailed to work on visits duty the following morning and the last thing I craved, was to suffer a crippling headache, at a time I was expected to be dealing with hoards of squawking infants racing around the place.

Chapter 11

Make Up And Ribbons

Chapter 11

Make Up And Ribbons

It appears that wagon wheels, pot noodles, Pringles, oh! and mars bars, are the staple diet during visiting times and it astonished me, that all most of the guests wanted to do, during their precious hour with their loved one, was to queue at the tuck shop hatch to buy hot chocolate, cake, bags of sweets and crisps or ice lollies; then spend whatever time was left arguing the toss.

Although many of the individuals coming into the visits hall managed to awaken the raging monster inside me, I was also fully aware, that for some people, visiting a prison can initially seem nerve wracking, and it's only natural to be concerned. We try our hardest to assure them that their relatives are being looked after, and we point out that there are services that offer non judgemental, emotional and practical support for families. However, we could only guess at how they would be coping, or how they were actually feeling, during their first experience of a prison visit.

I was very grateful that it had been a fairly quiet session, as the previous visiting hour had been a bit of a nightmare. Rose had seen one of the visitors clearly removing a little package from down her pants and transferring it into her mouth, the very cheek of it; she simply slipped it between her lips as she stood by the serving hatch. She then, paid for her teas and made her way back to her section. We immediately alerted the security duty officers and they approached the table just as she arrived back to it. They managed to hold back, as they observed her try to pass it by way of a kiss, it was timed so precisely and we watched in total amazement, as the team swooped before he had chance to hide it. Fortunately, it was all caught on CCTV and the offenders were removed.

At the same session, another one fiddled with her bra strap and as she passed her husband, she rubbed the back of his neck as she sat down. Just a few minutes later he started to fiddle with his T-shirt and was seen slipping a package down the front of his loosely fitting leggings. The cameras don't lies, and security had soon swooped and retrieved the goodies. Every day, these people take risks with their liberty, for a quick little fix, or a perhaps a few notes. Our searches are thorough, but, we obviously can't probe into underwear.

The Mums, wives and girlfriends all seem oblivious to the hefty sentences awaiting them should they get caught; either that or they didn't care. Everyone does a bit of ducking and diving nowadays, and some appear to think that a few misdemeanors will mean nothing to us, but, perhaps they should consider their families and how they would manage with another family member being banged up, especially if they have children. We understand they are under a lot of pressure to bring stuff in, but, the risks are really not worth it in the slightest, as very little can get past all the cameras, the guards or the dogs. Or us for that matter!

The visits hall was crammed with an array of interesting personalities, some were so used to coming, that they knew us all by name and others shied away quaking and darting their frightened eyes from one of the officers to another, as if they were afraid we would pounce on them. One elderly relative was spreading his bacteria by sniffing like a coke addict and then wiping his nose on his sleeve. I found myself really tempted to whisper "Hey, stay classy dude!" I kept my thoughts to myself, as we are not there to be rude to the visitors, we are there to assist them and guide them on their way

I couldn't divert my eyes from the pair of trousers with the nine inch bunch up the front. I recruited the aid of one of the male officers, and the bulge was found to be a quantity of spice, rolled up in a sock. Who knows whatever possessed him to be so blatant and to try his luck so recklessly. It was certainly some food for thought in this weird world of theirs that demands that sly chances are so blatantly taken. Of course, although the contraband had been intercepted and the offending visitor had been hauled off by the local police; I was made to suffer many hours of ribbing for looking at his cock.

I hate having to check out mouths, it's not just that sometimes they spit their chewing gum at you, or cough all over you, it's the huge toothless black holes that you almost fall into. Chewing gum is prohibited, it's classed as contraband, as it can easily be used to make moulds and occasionally, a clever-dick, will flatten it to the roof of their mouth thinking it won't be detected. Some of the characters are indescribable. Christ, sometimes I think I've seen far less make up and ribbons in a bloody circus! Nails like you would find on an ancient Chinese empress; on soft creamed hands that obviously do fuck all, and jewellery that would quite possibly drown you; if you went swimming in it.

We have now re-named the waiting area Silicone City, as there's often more than enough plastic to cover a football stadium and there are oversized titties and tattoos in abundance. Searching these people was a bit like swimming against the tide in a psychedelic time warp. I swear, that, if I have one more pair of perfectly formed bazookas shoved in my face, I'm going to flip a bloody gasket. Incidentally, I don't really appreciate replies like "No love just my tits!" or "Ha! Not for a long time love, I'm not that lucky." When I ask if there is anything inside their clothing? A few will hide things on their children and that's not a nice thing to witness, tiny babies with packages shoved inside their nappies, or infants with flat packages strapped to their small bodies, under the cover of multiple layers of clothing. Poor innocents, caught up in the selfishness of grown-ups!

One of the visitors who had some tobacco concealed in her hair-band said. "Well, I tried didn't I, tell him I tried. Hey, Miss, you can polish a turd as much as you like but you will never make it shine, sorry about that but they got to have a bit of splif to get them through their day innit! Tell him I will try harder next time Miss!" Well, it appears she might be right about the polishing thing, although, it appears you can roll it in a bit of glitter and that's acceptable.

I've removed so much contraband from collars, pockets and waistbands, that I've lost count. Some get turned away and their visit is revoked but some get prosecuted, it's not worth any of the risk and it's a sure fired way of getting into big trouble. Unfortunately, some of the wives, Mums and girlfriends are so scared of their men, that they simply do as they are told; there is still a lot of pressure put on them, even though their men are safely banged up. You will be surprised at how easy it is to intimidate and bully someone by letter or phone or even through a third party.

We never underestimate anyone, there are no level boundaries for some, they will try to pull the wool over your eyes and use all forms of bribery and manipulation. It gets easy to spot with experience and no means no where safety and security is involved. Sometimes we have to be brutally blunt. "No madam, you cannot wear your brooch with the six inch pin!" "No sir you cannot take your son's penknife in for him!" We simply look at each other and shake our heads at the lack of understanding. We try to explain that the rules are just like those at the airport but they still try it on. It's a sort of game with them and they think they can wear us down.

The blatant lack of decency never ceases to amaze me and a lot of the visitors arrive in the most inappropriate clothing and are sometimes turned away; as there is a very necessary dress code put in place to avoid any complaints. However, some of these people seem to have more strokes than a rowing team: I can't make head or tail of it all and I simply do what I need to do, to get them in to visit their men-folk. If they break the rules, then it's not our fault, it's their visit that they are gambling with, and they may have a very long wait for the next one if they have misbehaved.

Incidentally, we really do, actually try our very best to make the visiting hours an enjoyable and family friendly experience, as some of the men are away from their loved ones for a very long time and it's not nice. Our intentions are good, but, we still can't resist the observational humour.

Sometimes you get a kind of feeling that you shouldn't have let someone in, you can find nothing on them, but, you get a sort of intuition, and you just know they are going to initiate something that might cause some trouble. Obviously if someone is clearly under the influence of alcohol, or some other illegal substance, they will get themselves escorted out immediately, but I'm talking about a sort of sixth sense, that inevitably comes to the fore for no apparent reason. For example, one day, a very elegant woman who had arrived quite beautifully dressed, and acting normally, except for requesting a quiet seat in the far corner of the hall, was caught tossing off her husband under the table.

Another was seen masturbating, while her boyfriend watched with both hands down his leggings. It's unduly common for the visitors to wear no underwear and to open their legs for their other half to have a quick peek at their nether regions. They think it's a big joke, they think it's a bit of harmless fun and they think we are somehow oblivious to it, but, believe me we are on to it big style. After all, there are often small children in the room and it really is far from acceptable. There are other ways of relieving your frustration in private, so, perhaps we should set up a 'how to deal with self imposed celibacy leaflet' or offer advice on keeping your porn to yourself. Some don't seem to show the slightest bit of embarrassment when they get thrown out and they try it on time after time. They never seem to learn, but, all that happens is their visit gets cut short.

Some of the visitors like to talk a lot, you haven't got the time for trivial chit chat, but some think you are there to idle the time away and they dawdle and fuss on the way out. It can get really frustrating, especially if you are on an early lunch and you need to get away. Some are so upset that you have no alternative, other than to chat and offer them a kind word or two. However, there have been many times I really wanted to scream at some of them and advise them to make an appointment, next time they needed a consultation with one of our therapists. Sometimes, I really think I'm losing all control, as people just will not listen!

Chapter 12

The Culprit is Often Someone Close.

Chapter 12

The Culprit is Often Someone Close.

The senior officer's quote was really quite inspirational. "You should never argue the toss with a crazy fucker!" We all decided it was going to be the saying of the day. A few of the cellmates on the top landing of D Wing, had been in a fight, and by the time the officers had managed to open the door and get to them, one of them had been quite badly hurt. There was a make-shift tool found under the bottom bunk and it had been used mercilessly, it was the high price paid for being in a confined space with another prisoner if you pissed them off.

A lot of rough stuff went on behind the doors and the slightest little disagreement could often spiral into a serious assault; and however well the cell-mates get on, there is always the danger they will fall out over something trivial. It appears that the prisoner on the bottom bunk had been disturbed by the one on the top getting up to use the toilet and he had seen red, he had been hiding a razor glued into a pencil top under his pillow and he had lashed out at his cellmate, viciously, cutting his face and arms. He stood and laughed manically while the cellmate lay bleeding at his feet. Thank God, he had stopped flailing when the other prisoner became unconscious and had stopped fighting back.

The victim had needed serious hospital treatment, the duty nurses quickly patched him up and managed to stabilize him and fortunately, the ambulance was present in no time at all, he had undoubtedly had a lucky escape. It was not our job to judge the actions of even the most controversial individuals, but, sometimes we really lost our faith in a few of them. The prisoners sometimes had years of bad experiences and they took it all in their stride, they seemed to have somehow developed an innate resilience that transcended all their common sense and they were competent in the art of manipulation.

We knew there would be an investigation and it would result in several months of paperwork mayhem. It would mean all the officers working tirelessly on it until sheer exhaustion took on the form of sleep, it would be an epic struggle, as there would be all sorts of questions to answer, luckily, on this occasion, it was out of my remit, as I had no involvement with the event. My heart bled for those put to question, as I understood the difficulties of explaining an incident. Reporting, had been a major part of our training. It had to be spot on. There was no room for error.

I checked out a movement by the gate, Senior Officer Ferguson, could clearly be seen, silhouetted at the end of the landing; she stood there, quietly, with eagle eyed observation; she did nothing to intervene, and made no attempt to take the reins, I had nothing against her, personally, but, I was very much aware of her mud-slinging reputation.

It was a foregone conclusion, that if something went wrong, anyone in the vicinity could become her scapegoat, but, if it all went right, she would loudly proclaim to be the star of the show. It was a shame that her reputation caused some people to avoid her but it is what it is!

Seriously, she was reputed to be as shady as her shadow. Her reports were generally complex and engineered, as she somehow has a problem with her own self-esteem, and she manages to get ahead by putting other people down and raising herself up.

I averted my eyes from the Senior Officer, after all, we were in the middle of dealing with an ugly incident that was becoming increasingly physical, and we needed to brace ourselves for the onslaught. I had the back up of my colleagues and they had mine, and I was confident, that whatever happened we would deal with it, head on and with courage and diligence. Officer Ferguson, however, had soon revealed her nasty sting and instead of turning the chaos into order, she turned the order into chaos, she seemed to be afraid of her own success and had the knack of cocking things up, whilst on a desperate mission to do things right. It was a very interesting concept.

Every action and its response, had to be meticulously recorded and was scrutinized thoroughly. An individual had been very seriously injured and the blame would be apportioned. The incident had been out of our control, but the stress of confirming it would be immense. A very hard slog was ahead of us.

Everyone had been a bit concerned at the conflicting reports, there was far too much speculation and rumour and it was very unsettling for the officers involved. There was meeting after meeting and constant questioning by senior management; after a little while the earache gets excruciating. All you can do is stand your ground and keep telling them the truth. It comes with the territory, as even the tiniest white lie could tie you up in knots and cause you to lose both your job and your pension.

It's a saddening fact that sometimes even the most resolute, funny and warm officer, once full of banter and staunch vitality has become broken under the harsh scrutiny of the prison rules; through no fault of their own. They put their lives on the line every day, but, not only that; their careers are also constantly under strict accountability.

Average people would find it difficult to identify with, but a crudely formed home made shank, some contriband, spice and hooch, or whatever else there may be, can be used for bargaining and or threatening. It's a daily headache that is kept in check simply by good intel and observation. A major challenge is bullying, which can be anything from intimidation and physical abuse, to stealing and witholding food. Some appear oblivious to the forthcoming pain, when their debts are not met and others simply face it head on. The same demons keep calling out their names. The wiser ones keep themselves to themselves and get on with the daily regime without incident. It's a difficult challenge trying to keep everyone around you safe, when the odds are working against you.

Guess what I like about Mondays? Fuck all, the start of the week is always shit and this one was a hum dinger. A nephew of one of my neighbours had been brought in on remand following charges of rape and assault. I was already aware of some of the family history and I knew that he had suffered the worst upbringing possible. Someone like him can't be punished, all he knows of this life is pain, therefore any punishment, simply dissipates like water off a ducks back. You don't fully recover from that kind of childhood, the only time he was ever touched was to be beaten or abused. There had been no affectionate hugs, or Mothers love and something has to give, so its not really surprising that he was always in trouble or doing crazy or bad things. I anticipated that he would be a concern for the officers, he was a rebel and had a cruel streak in his nature.

He screamed obscenities at the officers, he told them that he knew he used to be a monster but he had changed, he promised he had changed for the better, the obvious inconsistencies in his stories were all too plentiful and offered up a diluted version of the actual events. We concluded that however much he protested his innocence, or insisted that he had changed, the truth could not be depended on. Whoever he said he was back then, definitely had not gone forever, he was already showing his true nature. The lad had led a fascinating life of crime and he carried a multitude of abuse and threat charges against him. In an act of rage, he lunged towards me and threw both his hands around my throat: I couldn't breathe, my lungs felt as though they would explode, as I fought for air. I tried to scream for help but he squeezed tighter. He hissed and spat profanities, as if to scare me into silence as he was cuffed and taken away.

I had to put in a conflict of interest report immediately, as he was known to me via his family, and he knew I was employed by the prison: I guessed he would try to get inside my head but I was more than determined not to be tainted by a shadow of a shadow. He sneered as he threatened the officers. "Maybe I could make a few calls and get someone on the outside to visit your families, to see your kids!" He made eye contact with me, and, I have to admit that fear began to manifest itself in me, but, I'm tougher than he thinks I am and I've got my colleagues to back me up.

We were leaning towards him as being a prime target on the wings, no one liked a rapist and there would be a queue waiting to give him a belt. The big question, was, whether there was anyone in the building who might hold any grudges and would be only too pleased to unlock their inner flow of negative energy, on such an abuser of women and more particularly of cruelty to small children. It was only prudent to put him in isolation for his own safety, as well as ours. All we could do, is manage the man well until he faced his trial.

Chapter 13

Invisible Endeavors

Chapter 13

Invisible Endeavors

The working dogs are quite amazing, they can detect the tiniest speck of contraband in an instant and it was thrilling to watch them at work. To untrained eyes it looked as if they were being hopelessly scatty, but, the end result is quite unbelievable, as nothing gets past them and there will be no escape for anyone that fancies taking the risk. The security and intelligence objectives are often reliant on the dogs and the random finds.

The dogs were running past the vans on their usual exercise in the yard and one of them stopped in his tracks. The handlers called but he refused to move. It was a sign that there was something amiss, so I watched as they searched around the area and located an orange. The fruit had some spice secreted inside it, and there was also a tiny mobile phone with a sim card and a charger. It was a brilliant find and with no intelligence involved. The head of security sent a search party around the perimeter to check for more. It appeared to be just that one, small piece of fruit but it was a great random discovery that had been prevented from going on the wings.

Not much gets through; however, we have to assume that some does. Idle minds are so adept and they have plenty of time to forge a plan. It's always a good feeling when there's an interruption to an illicit supply. It impacts on the safety and well-being of everyone. There is also the other issue, of course, which is the effect un-prescribed drugs, can have on prisoners who may be coming down from their medication, or drugs or alcohol, it's pretty scary and they need a lot of support. It's a delicate balance; the slightest disruption to the programme can set someone back for years and get them hooked again.

Each day brings new challenges which are met head on. The officers are vigilant and are constantly striving to keep the regime working as tightly as possible. The staff are the heart-beat of the prison and that beat must be maintained with gusto and nerve at all cost.

The Safer custody team worked tirelessly, often stumbling across covert transactions and conversations; that with good follow up and tactical and progressive leadership, could lead to a very clearly defined break-through. It's an uphill struggle for them and they are invariably on a high alert for any frightening and persistent behavior.

They often discovered clarity through the tiniest of misguided sentiments that could turn mayhem, into some sort of order. The analysts waited patiently and diligently for scraps of information, that would serve to prove their commitment. It's a constant struggle, of not only keeping the establish-ment safe but also to prevent any ongoing investigations from grinding to a punitive halt. Many of the criminal activities had been stumbled across by sheer chance and accidental discovery of coercive torment, would often become apparent in dialogue through phone calls and letters.

There is a variety of camouflaged control of emotional vulnerability and fear, it was ruthless and intimidating. It was evident, that some remained, in the clutches of the monster controlling them; even from the inside: There is an invisible hold on their emotions that they cannot seem to break.

They say they love them but they strive to dominate their every move. The word love gets flung around liberally and is so easy to say, but, love doesn't control you, love doesn't threaten you and love does not manipulate you! The immense power of possessiveness spread insidiously through every aspect of their existence, and they allowed it to happen. If they are told to do something from outside, they do it without question: A tennis ball full of tobacco, or an orange full of spice, the walls are high but a good aim can clear them. Thrown packages will occasionally get caught in the wire and can be brought down by the officers, but, without the aid of the sniffer dogs, there would be some confused with litter.

It would be such good birth control, if the women could only see this lot and the way they walk around inside. What a different image they would have of their men.

The lads trim each other's hair and sport their one style suits all, prison issue hair-cuts, as they strut their stuff. Once in a while some will presume to be legends but not many have the presence that so strong a title demands, and they act more like bell ends. They tend to take everything for granted and although they are trapped, they invent their own rules and will show very little fear. They share their ideas and resources and assume that their value as a person can only be determined, by how much money they can earn through illicit means. It's often quite easy to notice their little groups forming.

Embracing the best in the men is difficult and it can be a struggle to identify all the good things in an individual personality. There is usually something in their basic acumen, a little spark we can take forward into a skills pipeline to help them develop; however, it will sometimes remain a lost cause, as interest can't be forced.

Officer Alfie Drew, was beckoning to us for some assistance; he was engrossed in conversation with one of the recalls. "You don't own me so you don't get to tell me what to do; I'm a big martyr to my gang!" The officer smiled, before posing the question. "Do you really know what you have to be, to become a martyr to men?" "No; what?" "Dead!" The confused and angry inmate loudly shouted the odds, as he reluctantly turned towards his cell. "Fuck off and stop trying to show me up, I'm not stupid, I've got a lot of boys watching my back and I'm well thought of in this shitty hole. I've got plenty of followers and I can have you sorted out for good; you know what I mean?" If looks could kill, this would have been a perfect example. The prisoner backed into his cell and kicked the door behind him. It struck me that, maybe, the men have no other option but to try and shine as the leader in their ambiguous and empty lives. Unfortunately, it quite often creates some cause for concern, as the lost intellect may cast them adrift, when they are unable to beat an argument that makes no sense, and their normal retaliation is to then become violent and disruptive.

These extraordinary moments had a great impact on me; challenges were laid down on a daily basis and they would no doubt determine the welfare of the disconcerted individual, should his cloak slip a little. These inmates were not readily forgiving and for them, a good fight could relieve the boredom of a mundane routine.

Chapter 14

Tears From Your Little Sister

Chapter 14

Tears From Your Little Sister

The mail room is a hive of activity, there never seems to be a reason or sense in the incoming or outgoing mail. The content is mostly about missing and loving or family and pets and that's healthy. It helps with the wellbeing and loneliness issues, when good regular contact can be maintained. However, it's necessary to have a team of officers checking all the mail, as we never know what bits of intelligence can be gained from it. Regular money coming in can be a sign of corruption or bullying and harassment, or a word out of context can be a covert code or a signal to pass on. It's a necessarily thorough process as not even the slightest irregularity can be ignored.

Every single thing is suspicious, however irrelevant it may appear, it is scrutinized and dissected and the tiniest little piece of trivial information, can frequently be used to complete a huge puzzle that the security team may have been working hard on for several months. Letters, cards and e-mails flood in daily, in multitudes of shapes and sizes. The letters come from far and wide and from hoards of family members and friends: The worried Mum's and Dad's, the insolent brothers, the tearful sisters, cross aunts and uncles, sarcastic cousins, their lonely wives, abandoned lovers, etc. etc., and the list goes on. There are tears and accusations, excessive insults, rants and messages of support; a colourful array of sentiments that mostly fell on lazy and reticent eyes and were wasted, by sheer ignorance and a failure to respond. For some inmates, their letters are a lifeline, as many of the men miss their families, especially if they have long sentences, and the cards and notes from loved ones can mean the world to them.

The letters are also a good indicator of a prisoner's mental health or wellbeing and any depressive content noted, can cause the individual to be referred for support to the various health teams and counsellors. There are often many clues to be found to gauge this. Sometimes, depression can be found in the most beautiful poetry, that belies the hand it came from; ……………

The dark clouds have started to rain again.
Not all men are the same again.
The ones caught in the circle again.
It's taken its toll again.
I'm letting everyone down again.
The future is beyond my reach again.
Turn back the hands of time again.
There's no point in life again.
I might as well face it again.
I reached out but no one is there.

Notes like this, so beautifully written, in neat lines with deliberate and well thought out text, expresses the steadfast hand and seriousness of the content. Polished and thought provoking words that transmit a strong message. When compared with the usual light hearted tone of the mail from the prisoner in question, this type of letter quite clearly displays a different state of mind and needs instant action. You can't just change people's perspective on things but you can help set them on their feet again and there are many professionals in place to do just that.

The prisoners know that their mail is read and we all have to wonder if they are trying to influence us in some way, or cry for help through a legitimate source. It stands to reason that they enjoy a battle of wills, it helps them pass the time and God only knows, sometimes the time goes so slowly in here. Sometimes, the letters are highly amusing and sometimes they are disgustingly pornographic, nothing shocks us any more, we are all past that stage. It's the threats we act on decisively, as most of the time it's an artful warning to us that something is amiss or something is going to kick off on the wings: The operators in the mail room take everything seriously, so, we brace ourselves.

Perhaps they can't help it, as a lot of the men only know a life full of threats and violence. Many of them grew up with it, so to them it's normal behavior and their only way of communicating. All we can do is try to understand them and support them and pick up the pieces. I hoped I wouldn't get killed in the process, I was actually afraid to die; but only because I was scared that I would see the buggers on the other side and it would start all over again!

I'm going to have to face the fact, that, despite all my training, I readily have to admit, that although I was initially really struggling to come to understand all these diverse men and their choices in life; time spent with them brings clarity. Some of them were very hard to be nice to but you have to take a look at the whole picture. You need to reflect on their past, present and their future to understand it all. There are highs and lows for each one of us, including those detained, for whatever it may be, at Her Majesty's pleasure. There will always be new challenges along the way, but, I'm getting there! I'm building a sound foundation and learning to evaluate.

Chapter 15

Respectability

Chapter 15

Respectability

The contrasting arrivals stream in daily, a mixed bag of differing individuals, their emotions all over the place, sometimes it's due to the influence of illegal substances, but, mainly because of the new situation they find themselves in.

Some act crazy and some sparkle with the cheeky charm that gets them into trouble on the outside. Some will be quiet and not say much and some will try their luck and give a load of disrespect. There are many that will refuse to accept their fate and will thrash around with malice, thinking they are untouchable big guns. Then there are multitudes of sexual innuendos banded around in the presence of female officers and that can be quite tricky, but, there are usually plenty of formidable male officers to counteract it.

The worst that could happen, is that they make a big tit out of themselves and we know if we put chalk and cheese together they are just going to have to play it out, so, it's not really taken too seriously in the beginning and as soon as they realize the female officers won't bite, they tend to zip it and behave.

In amongst the chaos, an elderly tramp was being brought into custody. He was filthy, his trousers were stuck to his legs with dried on urine and his jumper was covered, with barely recognizable, smelly and mildewy remnants of his food. He looked as if he should have been sheep dipped before they let him in through the doors. They couldn't get him into the shower block; he fought against it and he screamed the place down. In the end they managed to get him to clean himself up, with the promise of a hot cup of tea and some biscuits. It's a very fine balance, when you have to allow for the choices, the standards of decency and the dignity of another human being. The effect of illicit substances can manifest in the most alarming ways. The poor old man was terrified, it is so real to the addicts, when they are under the influence and although you may think it's their own shortcomings that have caused their distress, some of the time it's their only escape from reality, as they know no other way and there but for the grace of God and all that stuff! It's the dealers that cause the most anguish and keep them hooked in their darkest misery.

He said he was being hunted down by a six legged devil with blood on his hands. He was very distraught, he pleaded with the officer. "Please, please, help me! I'm being hunted down; he's going to pop my eyes out. He's going to make me go blind for good this time, my eyes, my eyes, help me!" Sometimes humanity fades into the most pitiful desperation and will throw a completely curved ball our way.

It's not a pleasant experience to witness such wretchedness, in any individual and the officers sometimes have to recruit the help of the prison nurse, to settle the new arrivals down. Then, as much support as possible is quickly offered, particularly to those who are entering under duress.

Their lives are filled with twists and turns and it's not easy for them to choose the right path with a cool head, when they are caught up in the world of so much undue pressure. Some would inevitably succumb to those influences and become unwilling victims, as they participated in the game of chance. They are all given the benefit of the doubt, but, you maintain your guard at all times, they are like the fallen enemy that linger in the back of your mind

Chapter 16

The Hidden Horror

Chapter 16

The Hidden Horror

Prison doesn't deter them in the slightest, as many are more afraid of being on the outside, living at the mercy of the dealers and their debts. A cell can feel like a safe haven, considering the options of being homeless and forced to live on the streets. A hot meal, a warm blanket and a secure lock, is a welcome gift in their world of distrust and uncertainty.

It's a far cry from survival on the outside where there is plenty of help, if they want it but most of them refuse to be bothered, and will expect everyone else to do everything for them and then complain because they end up back inside. I suppose some of them want to quit but it's too much of a struggle and they lose their initiative. It's easier to give in and return to what they know, they are a complicated bunch. They all say they shouldn't be here, but, they should, really, as they can't be trusted to behave in the community. They develop an incredible sense of belonging and an almost family like bond in their profound ineptitude. Not all of them take everything for granted, some show immense resolve, however, courage is not contagious!

Loyalty is somewhat selective and can be easily bought and sold when there is no continuity. The newer ones, usually drift towards those they assumed would protect them and help make their stay as easy as possible. It can be difficult for them to keep their focus and we can never forget that these men are real people and their lives are very complicated; they will often become trapped in their own consequence and end up in a dark place. The qualities they possess are wasted, as they are of no value in a place like this. They will try to follow procedures, but, they don't really know how to, and we are sometimes left with a longstanding legacy.

When someone has taken their life under your care, you feel personally responsible, even though there was nothing that could have been done to prevent it. It's not an easy thing to come to terms with. There are not many organizations where you go to work only to confront someone who is intent on harming either themselves, or you. Some inmates will require a constant watch but you can never guess what is going on inside the troubled and hopeless minds, of those, who will say nothing and secretly plot their silent release. The war against suicide is a constant battle and every moment, of every day, is a huge concern. Some are unable to cry and have no release from their despair and some simply lack the will to go on; or are so overwhelmed by the pressures of their incarceration, that they feel they have no alternative when the days ahead weigh too heavy.

There are often no signs to expose intent, we carefully watch over those who may threaten, or give us reason for concern, however, they are so clever, even in the depths of their despair and it's often the ones that give little or no cause for worry, that leave us far too soon. It's a harsh and painfully brutal legacy of fear and failure to ask for help and it bruises our souls.

Chapter 17

Personal Disrespect

Chapter 17

Personal Disrespect

Oh damn it, a missed call from my Dad, it's not that I want to forget my roots, it's more that I don't really want to have to remember what I sprouted from; another nice day about to be ruined, oh, that's just terrific. My parents had divorced when I was in my early teens, after my Dad had buggered off with the young daughter of my Mum's best friend. Bloody seventeen years old and bonking the arse off my old man, I hadn't forgiven them, despite my Father's best efforts to bring me round to his way of thinking.

I decided to leave the return call for the moment, as I wasn't really in the mood for meeting the new flavour of the month. Since the divorce, Dad had really played the field; the previous one had actually got pregnant and was now a single mother at the age of 19. My Father had nothing to do with the child and didn't believe it was even his. I'm sure that one day she will get the DNA she needed for a bit of well deserved maintenance, but, she has simply gone her own way and she seems happy enough even without his support. The two before that, had simply lost interest in the idle bastard, once he had stopped showering them with flowers and gifts and had moved them in to his skanky flat to wait on him hand and foot.

I'm sorry to say, that I have complete and utter disrespect for my Father, nothing he can do, or say can excuse his behavior. I cried buckets for him when he first left but he didn't want to see me, he said I only complicated things. He said I should make sure I didn't give my Mother any worry, as she had more than enough on her plate, without me making it worse. I got used to only having my Mum around, but, Dad decided one day that it was important to keep in touch. There had been no cards or presents for years but then, all of a sudden he couldn't give me enough. The presents were meaningless to me; I am convinced that I would have appreciated them far more when I craved his attention, rather than now, when I've got so used to being without anything from him. It seems that the prick only contacts me if he wants me to pass on a message to my Mother, or to introduce me to his new woman. Oh, and sometimes he wants a bail out.

Mum has the ability to touch your heart and make it ache and Dad makes you feel like a useless imbecile. Any guilt I had for taking my Mum's side has long gone; the years of ridicule she suffered, has taken a toll on her health and I blamed my Dad for that. My Mother had been a fun-filled bubbly woman before he destroyed her soul. Now she has turned into my Nan, she looks much older than her 58 years and she just sits on the sofa in her dressing gown for most of the day; binge watching the telly and drinking cheap plonk. There are crocheted doilies all over the place and half knitted scarves and hats in a pile, on a stool at her side. It's comparable to living in a care home, except it doesn't smell of wee and disinfectant.

Nobody is going to be doing any more harm to my Mother, not even my Father, he refused to dance the dance, so he was thrown off the floor; it was as simple as that. Only the good die young and because of him, my beautiful Mother, had, at such a young age, become like the living dead. His issues were no longer our business and lack of cash-flow was his problem not ours.

I have always tried to keep my personal life private and very few of my workmates knew much about my home life. I think they thought that my Mum suffered from severe depression and they were right, so, I very rarely invited anyone home and no one questioned it. It would be too much for my Mother, in any case, and it wasn't worth upsetting her just for a quick coffee and a cake to be sociable. I always made an effort and went out for works events, as I wasn't entirely an anti-social recluse and it was perfectly fine to leave Mum on her own occasionally. She was happy with her own company and she simply put herself upstairs to bed when she had had enough of her knitting or the telly.

I think working at the prison distracted me from my own woes, as I often felt quite isolated at home, I spent as much time as possible with her, however, my poor, sad Mother had simply lost all her mojo and despite my constant coaxing and pleading, she has refused to socialize. I had learned a long time ago, to accept and support her choices and she was perfectly content in her own private and un-shakeable little world of knitting and magazines.

My Mother was nobody's clown; she had become infinitely sad after my Dad left her, as with losing him, she had also lost her best friend and her soul-mate. She had experimented with a dating agency on one occasion, after relentless nagging by yours truly, but, she said it made her feel even more worthless, to sit, showing off her wares to any Tom Dick or Harry, who just wanted a quick bit of nookie. There was nothing that would weaken her resolve to keep herself safe in her little cocoon of self preservation, away from the opposite sex. The woman was an enigma, a private and proud individual, I had a yearning in my heart for a life that was passing her by but she swore she was content and urged me not to worry.

Chapter 18

Passing The Time

Chapter 18

Passing The Time

It appeared that the prisoner's exclusive
new game, was seeing who could piss off
Senior Officer Perkins, the most, and the
pair in the end cell of the top landing were
pretty much the best contenders. They had
him chasing up and down the steps to their
cell constantly, but, to his credit, he kept a
cool head for quite a considerable time;
until it became undeniably clear to him,
that he was going to be their entertainment
for the day. There was a slightly comical
value to it but not from the point of view
of Senior Officer Perkins. He was livid.

We all need to laugh sometimes and the
dark humour that abounds within these
walls, is not always appreciated by those
inside them, particularly if it is directed at
them. I suppose we are such an easy target
for pranks and only the most experienced
of us were impervious to the game plans.
Officer Perkins had decided it was prudent
to take his frustration out on the raw new
recruits. "Where did that creature spring

from?" I whispered to Alyson, as Perkins stomped around, like a wounded elephant, in a vain attempt to salvage his wavering self esteem and I had to ask myself, if the man would suffer much, if I smashed his face in until it was unrecognizable, even to his own Mother! Shit, with thoughts like that I should be on the other side of the bars for my own good. I'm not usually a sadistic moron but sometimes my darker side invites me to have a little bit of fun and Perkins, was really kicking off, big style; at our expense. We tried really hard to apologize profusely for laughing but he told us to get back into our cages!

Poor Perkins, apparently, he suffers from chronic back pain, he had recently been divorced and was dealing with anxiety. He possessed a cruel wit and his tongue lashings were second to none. We just assumed it was the pain that made him that way and when he was dancing around the room on one of his rants; we actually felt quite sorry for him, even though we delighted in the entertainment of it. The accusations and questions being launched around the room were resounding on us all and the more aggressive and pushy the questions were becoming, the more highly charged and grotesque the scene did by reflection. Officer Brown then concluded, that enough was enough and he screamed at Perkins to pack away his fucking ego. This was the moment that the atmosphere became quite menacing and luckily Senior Officer Marksham arrived and showed an inherent resolve in diffusing the situation.

"Perkins! all you do is criticise and insult my officers, you do nothing to support or help them, you are like a bloody spoiled child and they are no less significant on these wings than you are. You rummage through their personal lives and mock their decisions, while all the time ranting and raving about irrelevant rubbish. If you have a problem with any of us, then go and see the Gov right now!" The bar had been firmly set and Marksham turned and marched away, as Perkins stomped away towards the landing door, presumably to make his way to the Governors office.

One of the inmates shouted: "Hey, Miss, can I borrow your cell keys to lock up that mad fucker, cos he's doing my bloody head in, oh, for fucks sake!" Some of the inmates are so impatient, although I have no idea why, as they have nothing to do and nowhere to go.

Everyone laughed and it only served to infuriate Perkins even more. "You lot will suffer if you don't pack it in, if you are making plans for the weekend, you had better forget about them!" We didn't want to make any more waves and none of us wanted to be called in for extra duty on the weekend, so we settled down knowing that the Perkins incident would be the topic of conversation at lunch. We crossed our fingers in the hope that he would have calmed down before the end of the day.

Most of the prisoners' little pranks are so common they go unnoticed and whatever happens during a shift is irrelevant, as we are paid for our time and not the event. The pranks or silly games will be quickly forgotten. However, sometimes, there will be the one, that will still make you giggle long after the incident.

Chapter 19

Take Care

Chapter 19

Take Care

We've been through far grimmer periods than these. It comes with the territory that you put yourself at risk. You simply have to be resourceful and watch each other's backs and remember your groundwork.

We have to undergo regular and updated training and if we failed miserably, would have to answer to our line managers, It felt like an eternity sat on the grey chairs, with the threadbare bits at the front, where the material of the seats had been worn away by innumerable, enthusiastic, new recruits, as they shuffled on their attentive arses, whilst sitting and listening endlessly to many spell-binding lectures. I sincerely hoped the day ahead would be interesting and the officer in charge was not going to be too hard on us.

"Right you lot, can you make tea and can you talk a load of bullshit? They are the only two requirements I need from any of you lot today!" I heard the chirpy sound of

Senior Officer Jameson and I knew it was going to be a good training session. He was one of the good guys, one of the favourites that everyone had a lot of time for. He was approachable and helpful and he didn't make you feel like you were useless, or would never get anywhere; or ever achieve anything. His ego was intact and there were never any raw digs at us newcomers. He was always more than happy to furnish you with his wealth of experience and was quick to praise you for trying your best. It was a good call. Assisted by the lovely Officer Donaldson and the funny Officer Mortimer, Senior Officer Jameson commenced with the onslaught.

Even after ten weeks of in depth training, the momentum can catch you by surprise. The tiny gold studs flew from my ears, as I speedily donned the helmet during the fire hood training. "What the fook is going on in here?" Officer Donaldson, flipped up the visor and shoved my hair to the side so that I could see. "You are like a bloody Wookie, good effort but tie your bloody hair up and let's start again is it?" I did it again, but properly this time around and we continued the exercises without further complications. Regular and up to date training is an absolute necessity, as you can very easily become complacent and think you are ok just because you did it right the first time. However, practice makes perfect, as you can get really rusty, so it's good to keep things fresh in your mind, we were all on the same page with that and we took the training seriously.

The training room was crammed full, of mostly eager and attentive newbies, who, just like me, were sat glued to every word uttered by the senior officer. It was going to be a busy day and although we knew all the radio techniques, were confident with Control and Restraint procedures and had had it drummed into us that restraint is the last resort; We were all still nervous. We knew how to separate and judge a lot of issues and how to recognise paranoia and we understood the Local Strategies, etc., but, we soaked up the information again and completed all the practical scenarios with flair. However, without a doubt, our sheer lack of experience shone through.

We all longed for the day it would become second nature to us. Nevertheless, we all got praised and encouraged throughout the process and each of us left with a satisfied grin.

As we finished for the day, we noticed Officer Truman walking round with an A4 clipboard under his arm, thinking it made him look busy. You couldn't make it up. It could be quite unsettling, to know that one of the security guys, cupped his keys in his hand outside the offices, so that you couldn't hear them jangling as he held his ear to the door to eavesdrop. All we could do, was to turn a blind eye, when he was caught grappling with his bunch of keys, in his attempt to hide his nosiness. His sloth like movements across the wings were becoming a familiar daily occurrence and the only thing he left in his wake; was a trail of gripes, from those of us who may have said something we shouldn't have.

Those who don't understand the concept of working in a prison, would find it hard to accept, but, it was his job to keep the establishment safe and after all, as head of security, he has to be the most profound analyst in the building. It was in his nature to be suspicious and sometimes, with very good reason. If we were speaking out of turn then it was our fault, not his. He was a sort of, likeable pain in the arse.

I was getting used to the quirky ways of the people I worked with and I loved them for their individuality, although, there was the occasional one that simply craved the power a uniform commands. Most of the officers were plain and simple individuals walking the walk and talking the talk and there were not that many I wouldn't be grateful to cover my back. However, there could always be the odd one that would make you think twice.

For example, one of the older officers who had been at Scupton for several years but had never worked up through the ranks, or showed any desire for promotion; stayed happy to do the mundane sitting down jobs. Then there were those who might be overly aggressive and those slow to react. Despite their lethargy, I did not think for one moment, that any one of them would fail to back up their colleagues. It takes all sorts and it's the variety of personalities that make the job interesting and pulls us all together. There is an unwritten alliance between us all to protect each other. It's just, that, some of us are a bit quicker than others to move our butts.

It stands to reason that there will be in-house disagreements and not everyone can sing from the same hymn sheet. It's not in our nature as humans, to like everyone else and one of the officers had rubbed me up the wrong way from the start. I don't know why exactly I found him so irritatingly rude. I think it was purely a case of mutual dislike. There was nothing I could do about it, except secretly imagine his genitals were searched thoroughly, on a regular basis. I mean, he probably has a party in his hands, but, no-one else is invited. For those who haven't got a clue what that might mean, it's a polite way of calling someone a big wanker. God only knows what he thought about me, but at least I was civil and didn't return his disapproving looks.

I find it uncomfortable being in the mess room when he happens to be around, as the only conversation he has, is about all his conquests on numerous dating sites, he's obsessive about dating and pretends to be meeting up with all sorts. Trouble is, he is often spotted alone and nowhere near the places, he had defiantly claimed to be at and I wished he would just hurry up and find someone nice to tell the truth about and get on with life. I really do believe there's someone for everyone, so he might get lucky after all. Anyway, as it isn't really any of my business. I just listen and nod, although, I will freely admit, that I usually found myself wanting to scream. "Stay if you want but for fucks sake, just stop talking!" His fantasy life defied the lies he spun to anyone who would listen.

Most of the time passes by calmly and without incident. The nastiness is rare and despite the greyness around us, there can often be a sincerity and light-heartedness. Every moment will count in this diverse environment and the simplest thing like a pretty butterfly through the bars, or a little bird eating bread out of your hand, can bring colour and light into an otherwise mundane day. The slightest little thing can cause great excitement and we've heard screaming like a frightened infant at the dentist, that has caused us to go running, only to find an injured sparrow that has flown into a cell and been rescued by the men.

Chapter 20

Good Judgement

Chapter 20

Good Judgement

As officers, we are constantly putting our lives on the line and we are tested to our limits on a daily basis; out of sight of the public eye and in an increasingly volatile and un-predictable place.

The staunch, dedicated men and women, walk the landings, with no idea what they can expect, as they unlock the complicated stories hidden behind a door. They have long since learned how to harness their personal feelings and to treat their charges with dignity and fairness. It's one of the most versatile and demanding jobs and they have to be vigilant and hold a nerve of steel. My mission is to learn to be just like them and to take everything in my stride, without fear or aspersion.

It takes skill, tenacity and good judgement to implement the knack of knowing when to take a step back and to be mindful of choosing the right battles. A lot of effort is made encouraging the inmates to focus on their strengths and abilities, instead of on their anger and contempt, for the officers, the police and the law courts that placed them with us. A short sentence doesn't seem to effectively deter them from their self destructive behavior; in fact, it can often make them more rebellious and determined in their intent. A good officer can persuade the inmates to leave their emotions behind them and can encourage them to strive towards being the best possible version of themselves.

It's surprising how many will find that they are stronger than they ever believed they were and will end their sentence on a positive and forward thinking note, simply with good management.

Despite the theory that prison can be an intolerant place to exist, I've found very little evidence of it here at Scupton. My colleagues and the prisoners, work in a respectful harmony, most of the time and there is a good rapport across all gender, sexuality and race, so I think, perhaps the media, or simple assumption plays a big part in those opinions, as the diversity and tolerance is intact. Racism, most certainly does not have a place here, as after all, if you crack a white egg the contents are the same as if you crack a brown one and we are all in it together!

The people in our care should always feel free from fear of retribution and if they are offered genuine support and encouragement; the likelihood is, that a respectful and safe environment can be achieved and behaviour can often be contained without physical intervention. Good support can alleviate risks to the establishment. I still have so much yet to learn and I am often astounded by the success of my colleagues in their endless quest, to maintain a calm and balanced environment.

When a serious incident may require our normal regime to be shut down, specialist teams are brought in and fixed posts are deployed. The establishment goes on total lockdown and high alert and it can have a lasting effect on the entire team depending on the outcome. There are many scenarios that might require this and when the shit actually reaches the fan and the spray is real, it's imperative that the fundamentals are in place. We are constantly challenged with random drills called at short notice, intense and real time scenarios, which run alongside in-depth training. The efficient management of this is paramount. It's the full central nervous system of the prison service; it's where the buck stops. I have yet to be involved in a real incident but the thought of it makes my toes curl and I hope I keep my focus when it happens, as it inevitably will, it's bound to. It happens to us all at some point during our service.

My training has prepared me well for all eventualities, however, when it's put into practice it's a totally different story; it's as scary as hell and you have to have a tight arse to make it through. Messing things up is not an option when you have the added responsibility of looking out for all those around you, as well as yourself. Although it's pretty terrifying, it will teach you what sort of person you really are and it will soundly challenge your competence.

I'm not giving up, I'm going to get where I need to be, I am determined to overcome whatever obstacles I may face, and there is nothing that can be thrown at me that will shrink my resolve. Brave talk, I know and I imagine all the trainees before me, have spouted exactly the same, however, seeing the officers for real has inspired me to follow in their footsteps and I'm more than determined not to fail.

Chapter 21

Team-building

Chapter 21

Team-building

Never in a million years, will I be going on another one of our group team building weekends. The assumption had been that it was going to be an absolute ball; with pool tournaments, karaoke and plenty of alcohol, however, our lot seemed to have different ideas and they were all complete light-weights.

The mini bus ride had been fun, we sang and played silly games but as we checked into our hotel rooms, an invisible vacuum appeared and preceded to suck away the personalities from everyone and they all started bitching and moaning.

The very first night, was a disaster, there were 13 of us, unlucky 13 as it turns out. Two of the younger, single officers were trying to get off with the only girl in the building and a big fight kicked off. They managed to knock the hell out of each other and whilst they were fighting over her; the attractive blonde had buggered off with someone else. They got even more pissed off after that and sparred with each other throughout the entire night; they just wouldn't let it go.

There were no cues on the snooker or pool tables and nothing remotely recognizable on the juke box. The barman looked like he had just walked off the set of the living dead and the place was deserted; it was as though we had arrived at a sort of ghost-town Ibiza on zombie night.

The usual insults abounded, but, they were just getting more and more personal as the night went on: Of course, you need a bit of light banter and I'm more than prepared to pay the price with my vanity, however, I'm not prepared to sell my soul as well. I did, just about manage, to give everyone as good as I got but I am nowhere near the league of the others.

Then there was Royston, he had originally declined to come away because his new wife was expecting. He managed to stay drunk for two whole days and was chasing young skirt every five minutes. He didn't manage to get his leg over once, despite the fact he had spent all his money on a prostitute, he said he just couldn't get it up due to him being so intoxicated. I quickly decided that I would prefer to end up as a lonely old spinster, than be lumbered with an idiot like that. The solitude wins hands down for me. Oh yes, loneliness or dick-head? No contest!

He thinks he's somebody, but, really, can you imagine if he actually was? He likes to think he's rather cool but he hates any responsibility and is a coward in a fight. As trouble is coming in the back door, he runs out the front! He will have to censor all his stories for his grandchildren when he is older, in order to avoid looking like a bloody great fool.

His long suffering wife is actually really nice, perhaps a little prim and nothing like you would expect to be matched with him. She had once declared that in her opinion, "Most new marriages don't last because you can't really see each other during the day and you can grow apart without the constant affection if you work shifts, but, we are tight and there is nothing that will pull us apart!" Oh my God! She was so wrong. However, we couldn't tell her that most new marriages don't last, because husbands like yours are absolute twats. I really think she would smash his world's best husband mug over his head, if she only knew.

I was painfully single and I knew it, but, I was staying that way! I had no intention of becoming someone's doormat. Suddenly, my attention was drawn to the rest of the group, as they were howling and throwing beer mats.

Patrick started his insane nonsense, doing his annoying elephant impression, where he turned his pockets out and undid his zip. He didn't appear to realize that some people tend to take offence when you get your knob out and wave it in their face! We all gave him a load of grief but he was expecting it and he dealt with the insults by simply giving us a cheeky smile and a shrug of his shoulders. He kept his cards close to his chest about his personal life, but, I'm sure he has a very sick secret.

The infinitely funny and adorable Megan, whom, by the way, unwittingly manages to offend everyone in her path, arrived late as usual, and her entrance on this occasion was no exception. Bloody hell, her shorts looked as if they were sprayed on her and believe me, the last thing you want to see coming towards you, was the outline of stubbly labia! Her pretty face looked like she had been doing painting by numbers on it and she wobbled ungainly on her overly high platforms. She provided us with so much unintentional amusement; she was a walking disaster but we loved her dearly.

Lana was trying to stand up straight; she had enjoyed a few too many glasses of prosecco. Her dress was far too tight and she was having a real battle with her bits. Karen went to her rescue, before we all settled down to a mass debate about our behavior and we all agreed, that we really needed to grow up.

We saw off a few final drinks before we decided it was bedtime and Tom sang on the karaoke until they threw him off.

It was a strange encounter and what had I been reduced to? I was worried that I may insidiously be becoming a binge drinker? I woke up in a strange room, I could see two faces on the telly and I was lying on my side in a pool of spew, that had missed the bucket that had been carefully placed at the side of the bed, by God knows who. I knew I would have to brace myself for the ensuing fallout and that was my own fault. I really hoped that I hadn't ruined the night, as I couldn't remember a bloody thing. I really felt the urge to send a group e-mail to my colleagues. "Please don't ask me to come the next time you decide to go for an expensive and shit weekend. I am busy for the rest of my life!"

Despite the few minor incidents, we all actually managed to have a whale of a time and the team-building exercise, did eventually go down in history as a great success; if only to confirm that we were all in it together.

If you can't stomach the leg pulling, you have absolutely no chance of success in an environment like prison; the harsh reality of incarceration can play silly games with a troubled mind. Some of the newcomers are probably a bit guarded and they need to find someone on their own level, to draw their emotions to the surface. You have to learn how to survive and not take the insults personally and it takes a little while. There is no escape and being quiet won't really protect you from the banter, which can sometimes be very harsh. So, we all join in and it's strangely healing, it's almost like possessing your very own venting tool, particularly for someone like me, as my old bullies still lived in my head.

Whatever obstacles or personality clashes we perceived, we were sure that with our sound sense of teamwork, there was not a single thing we would fail to achieve; in our contrary but tight knit little group.

Chapter 22

The Price Of A Prank

Chapter 22

The Price Of A Prank

I remember the first time I met Tom, his playful alarm button prank was actually pretty awesome, if I'm honest. Apparently he does it to all the new recruits and we all fall for it. The Senior Officer wasn't quite so amused and warned him not to do it again, or he would be put on report. "I swear to God Tom, if you had something to do with this again!" He was incensed and gallons of his saliva flew in every direction, as he screamed "You are funny, but you are going to be dead funny if you don't pack it in mate?"

His anger was understandable, as after all, in a place like this, an alarm going off is something that would normally mean big trouble and the joke was not to everyone's liking; particularly when they have just legged it from the furthest part of the jail, to arrive breathless and expectant; only to find a red faced newbie and a couple of officers rolling around in fits of helpless laughter.

Tom got called away to see the Governor later that afternoon and we haven't seen him since.

We think he may have misunderstood the consequences of his infantile actions but this time, lady luck had left the room and he had paid the price with his job. We all tried to rally round but the Governor was having none of it. It had happened far too many times for his liking and he had had enough. We are each responsible for the protection of everyone around us. There is no safety net when you are caught playing around with safety or security. We found out later, that he had been suspended then transferred at a lower grade.

He never contacted any of us, or returned our calls, we think he thought we failed to support him but we didn't, he wouldn't let us! We loved Tom; we didn't want to lose him, either as a colleague, or a friend.

We were left with a really horrible feeling deep in our guts; it had never entered our minds that the reprimand would go so far. Tom has stopped all contact with each and every one of us and we mourned the loss of somebody extraordinary in the team.

We might as well face it, however hard we work and however decent we are in our roles, there is always a price to be paid for the slightest lapse of our concentration. Human thoughts, words, feelings and the smallest of actions can have a marked effect on those around us, and, however well meant, innocent, or entertaining they may appear, they can sometimes become embodied by very negative events.

Tom had been made an example of; he had been given the holy shit package. It was the Governor's way of pulling us back into the reality of our work and the seriousness of our roles. We were given a hard lesson about the consequences of any misconduct and it resounded on us.

We never know what's around the corner and we constantly kept in mind, that there, but for the grace of God, could go any one of us. For some of the men it wasn't really a question of, if, it was a question of when they were going to end up getting caught, as their crimes were prolific and the odds were always against them. We all make mistakes and some of us pay more than others it's as simple as that. If you break the law you will get punished. It can't be considered too harsh, it's just justice. We could never tell what personalities were going to come through the door, or what impact they may have on the staff or their fellow prisoners, it was a free lotto of our human nature. Their crimes are not always all about money; sometimes it's about having control.

It's not simply a case of a universe full of evil vagabonds waiting out there; it was more a case of people dabbling in things they shouldn't have dabbled in. A mix of gamblers, fighters, thieves, bullies and all sorts of controlling, power crazy egos that knew no better and brought unrest into the establishment. We were all there to see to their needs, they had already been judged and their liberty had been lost. It's not possible to judge any path if you haven't already walked it and it wasn't our place to do that. They had already been before a judge and jury!

It was a while before we started to play pranks again but we are still mindful of the consequences. I suppose it's ingrained in our make up, to work hard and to play hard and there is an infinite bond between us all. With each new day we can witness happiness, sadness, tragedy and euphoria.

We deal with everything head on, just as we were trained to do. Occasionally there is unrest but in general it's short lived and not too serious. I think it's a job that only certain people can sustain and you have to be able to deal with a smoking gun when all you have is the smoke. I stand back in awe as some of the brilliant deductions are made and tragedy is stopped in its tracks. I feast on the resilience, the patience and the integrity of my fellow officers, as they go about their daily business of keeping the prisoners safe and content during their incarceration. It's a hard fact that tempers will occasionally flare, as, after all, we are only human and we are meant to roam free; but we walk the wide landings, with a courage and honour; that very few will comprehend.

I have just passed my probation and I wouldn't want to work anywhere else or with anyone else, our team is tight and supportive. I've swung around numerous learning curves and found my own way. There is still the issue of Officer West but it's nothing I can't handle and there are now witnesses, incidentally, he seems to have backed off a bit, after a few kicks in the nuts! I would still be happy to see him crash and burn, but, I have to remember, its teamwork and all our differing quirks, favorable, or not, are what make us the unique and productive group that bands together, despite our diversity. We are all dependant on each other. We know each other and we can feel confident and ready for anything that may be sent our way. Likes and dislikes are irrelevant in our line of work, we simply watched out for each other, unbiased and sound.

The work is really challenging with long hours and plenty of stress. Yes, an awful lot of lessons have been learned on the way and a lot of ground has been covered. The ethics are steadfast and the work is more rewarding than anything else I have ever experienced during my working life. We have our challenges and we have our beautiful and rewarding moments. It's a commitment like no other and we learn to take everything in our stride. We become far more in tune with our five senses and we understand the true meaning and value of togetherness.

Although we laugh and make light of our time within these dismal grey walls, there is hope and comradeship that will never be found elsewhere. The lessons I have learned along the way, will no doubt remain ingrained permanently. I have finally earned my first stripe, so, I'm now a fully fledged prison officer and of that I'm immensely proud.

Living the Dream on G Wing

Warning

This publication contains adult content and strong language.

The sun may have gone in but I am still shining

245

This fictional story about prison, features the high's and lows of the daily routine of prison officers, as they work in a confined and secure establishment.

The sometimes lighthearted situations and comedic events only mask the dangers the officers face as they enter the gateway into a mysterious and unpredictable place.

The story is told through the eyes of a new recruit, as she finds her way through her probation and any resemblance to anyone living or dead is purely coincidental

Each new day resounds in the steadfast comradeship found behind the walls of HMP Scupton and demonstrates the extra-ordinary affiliation between the officers, the individuals they are responsible for and others they may have to work with. The humour, although dark and comedic, transcends the diversity of the job and the challenges and colourful moments that are apparent within a secure environment, that few will experience.

248

Cover Design:
Book Covers.//FrinaArt

The prison officers unlock a new story every time they open a cell door and each day holds uncertainty in a hostile and volatile environment.

ISBN: 97817013251

Other Books

The Valley Beyond
A Nightingale Sang
Perhaps it was Jane
Five Nights in Ponty
The Night we Died
Handbags at Dawn

Bite size books written in an easy to pick up and put down style

Author

Sheila Cooper
Sheila, was born in the valleys of South Wales,
she enjoys writing in an easy to pick up and put
down style using short chapters and a quick flow
in cross genre subjects. Sheila Cooper is the pen
name of Irene Husk.

Thank you, to everyone who supported me, as I wrote this story, particularly to my ever patient and tolerant husband, Dean.

It's not really that easy to live a positive life with negative thoughts. If you don't leave your past where it belongs, it will destroy your chances of a happy and successful future.

So live for what today has to offer and not for what yesterday has taken away.

Printed in Great Britain
by Amazon

72901539R00156